DINO

A WELCOME BOOK

EDITIONS
New York

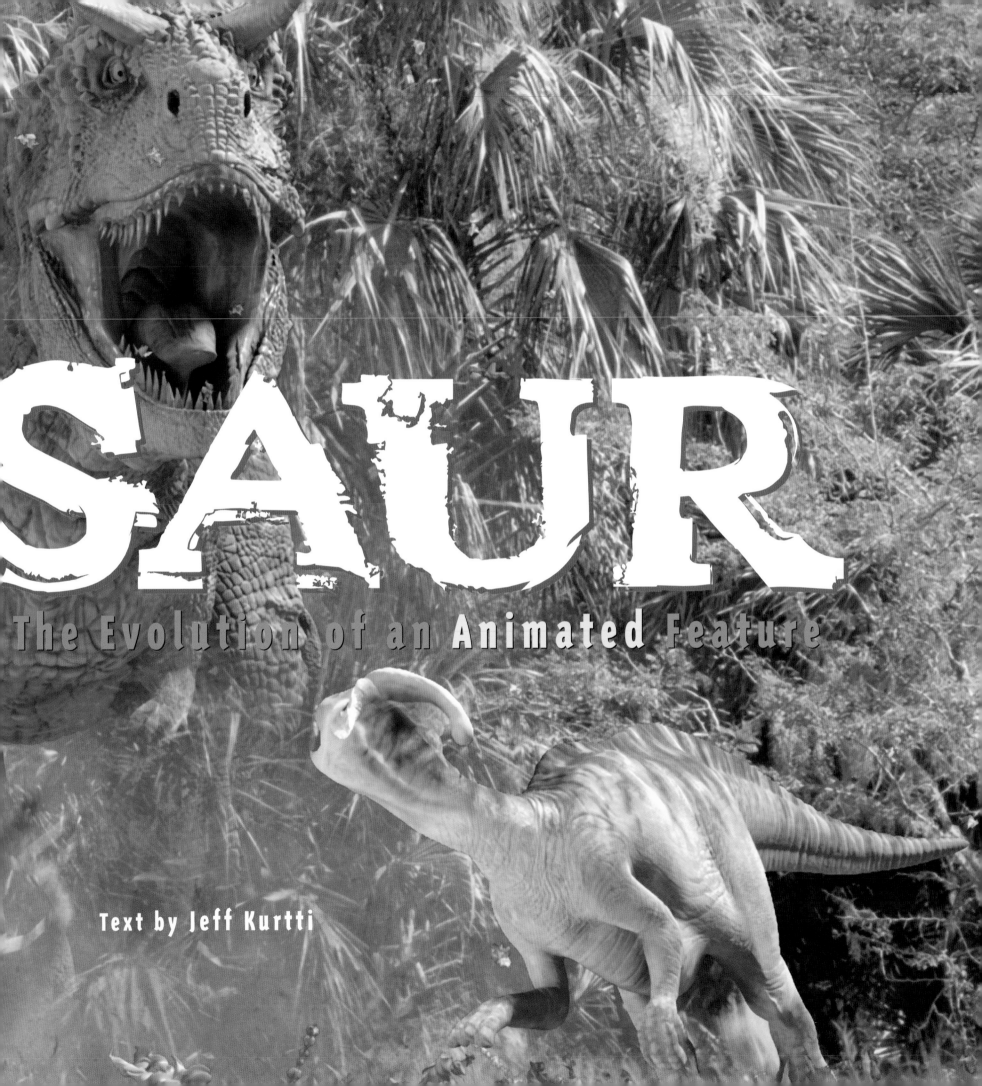

SAUR
The Evolution of an Animated Feature

Text by Jeff Kurtti

"If you can visualize it, if you can dream it, there's some way to do it."—Walt Disney

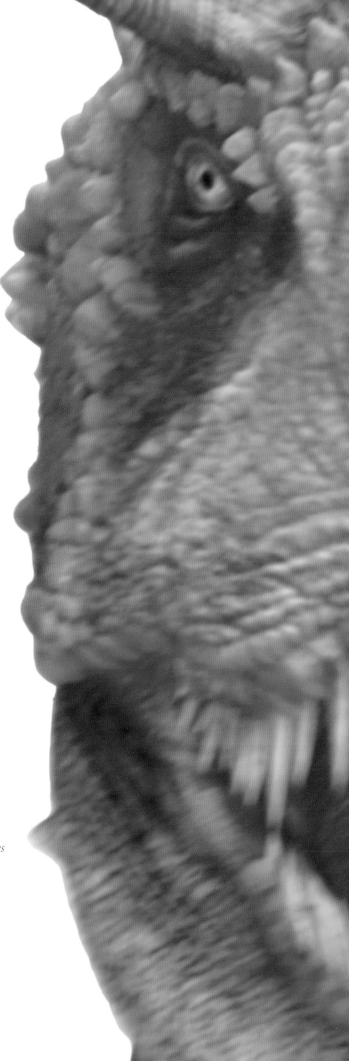

Adapted from
Walt Disney Pictures Presents *Dinosaur*
Directed by Ralph Zondag and Eric Leighton
Produced by Pam Marsden
Coproduced by Baker Bloodworth

For Michael Pellerin
—JK

Copyright © 2000 Disney Enterprises, Inc.

Produced by:
Welcome Enterprises, Inc., 588 Broadway
New York, New York 10012

For Welcome:
Designer: Jon Glick
Project Manager: Alice Wong

For Disney Editions:
Editorial Director: Wendy Lefkon
Senior Editor: Sara Baysinger
Associate Editor: Rich Thomas

For information:
Disney Editions, 114 Fifth Avenue
New York, New York 10011

Library of Congress Cataloging-in-Publication Data
Kurtti, Jeff.
 Dinosaur : the evolution of an animated feature/Jeff
Kurti.
    p. cm.
 ISBN 0-7868-5105-8 (alk. paper)
 1. Dinosaur (Motion picture: 2000) I. Title.

PN1997.D495 K87 2000
791.43'72--dc21   00-20297

Printed and bound in Japan by Toppan Printing Co., Inc.

10 9 8 7 6 5 4 3 2 1

Production stills from the opening scenes of Dinosaur:

PAGE 1: *A mother iguanodon stands watch over her eggs.*

PAGES 2–3: *The dinosaur Nesting Grounds: a Garden of Eden.*

PAGES 4–5: *A carnotaur explodes through the trees and shatters everything in its path.*

THESE PAGES: *Carnotaur . . . a mouth full of teeth and a bad attitude.*

OVERLEAF: *One egg from the iguanodon's nest remains miraculously undisturbed.*

Contents

SOME THINGS START

AND SOME THINGS

BUT SOMETIMES THE

CAN MAKE THE

OUT BIG,

START OUT SMALL . . .

VERY SMALL.

SMALLEST THINGS

BIGGEST

CHANGES OF ALL.

FOREWORD

OPPOSITE: *Visual development art of Aladar with a lemur friend by Thom Enriquez.*

The most significant observation I can make about the success of our movies is that they are all built on an eloquent and universal thematic foundation. Whether it is *Beauty and the Beast* ("Don't judge a book by it's cover"), *Aladdin* ("It's who you are on the inside that counts"), or *The Lion King* ("You must be responsible to your community, not just to yourself"), if you look at the success of these movies, much of it is in the *story* we've chosen to tell.

Dinosaur continues that legacy. The story of *Dinosaur* is a journey of self discovery—what you must do to survive, the responsibility we have to those around us, the ability to change the world by working together. These stories are based on fundamental values, in any language, in any culture.

The art of storytelling lies in making the characters appealing and compelling. That's what makes an audience want to spend time with them. In live action, great actors help accomplish this. Animators are quite simply great actors. They're often called "actors with a pencil," but in the case of *Dinosaur*, their pencil is the computer.

As the computer gets more powerful, as the tools become more accessible, and as the animators become more familiar with the tools, using the computer to create great acting has become an art in itself. Part of the success of *Dinosaur* is that the technique disappears as audiences are captivated by these fabulous animals that they believe are real—dinosaurs with credible personality, emotion, and intellect.

It has always been the ambition of The Walt Disney Company to do things that have never been done before—to surprise the audience at all turns in terms of technique and storytelling. That was Walt Disney's mission—he did things no one had ever seen or heard before. *Dinosaur* certainly continues that promise of innovation.

With *Dinosaur*, we were able to adapt a live-action cinematic vocabulary—backgrounds, staging, lighting, camera movement—and add great animated characters. The result is something quite exciting—live action and animation coming together to create a whole new genre with limitless potential for storytelling.

I believe the Disney name stands for excellence, and value, and uniqueness, and peerless storytelling. Because of that, our goal is always to do it better, to push the edges of storytelling, technology, and characters, and to *keep* pushing, to places we've never been before. We may not get there, but if we don't shoot for the stars, we'll never succeed.

Peter Schneider
Chairman, The Walt Disney Studios

11

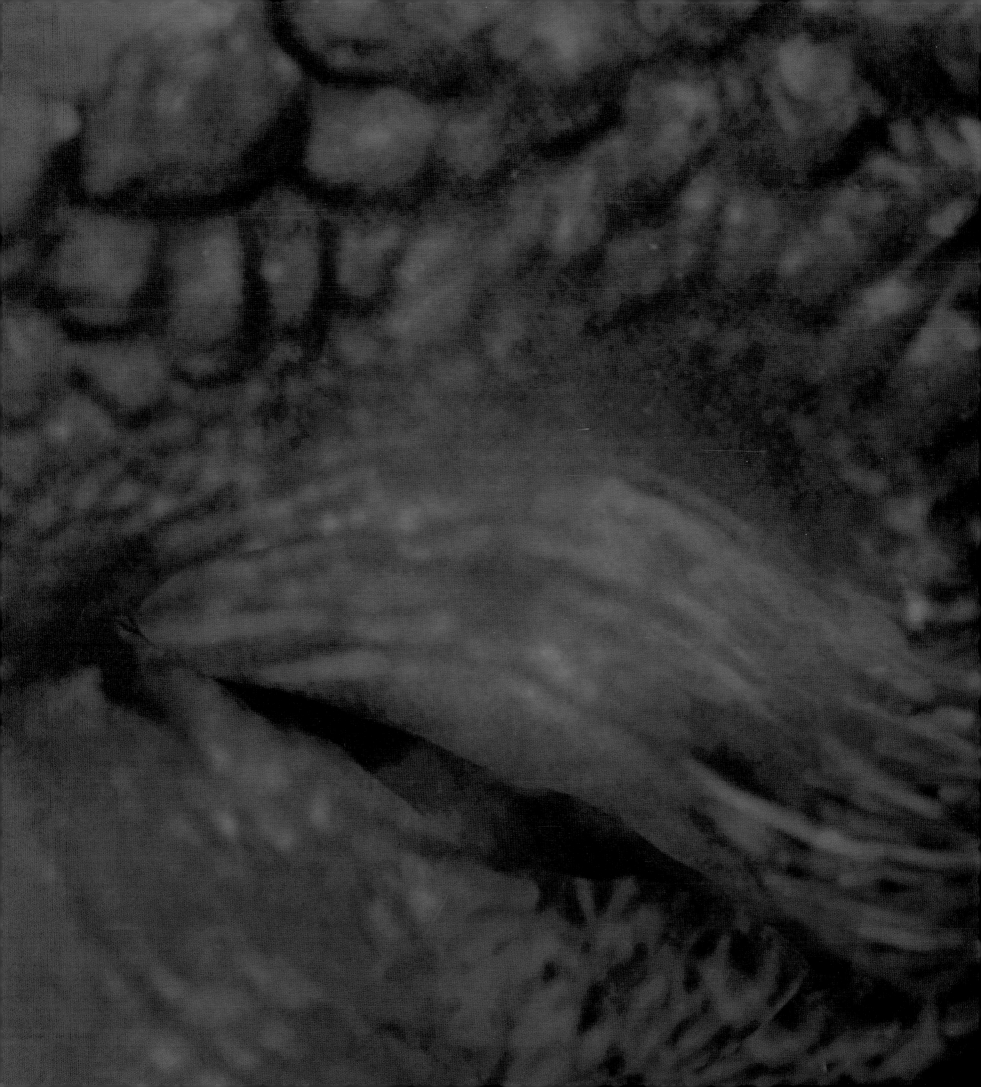

PART ONE **THE BIRTH OF A NOTION:** THE "PREHISTORIC" *DINOSAUR*

IN THE BEGINNING...

Doing a film with living, breathing, credible dinosaurs as the main characters is a very exciting notion. When the idea first came up a

"Every oak tree started out as a couple of nuts who decided to stand their ground." —Unknown

The opening scene of Dinosaur *from inside Aladar's egg: vague shadows in dim light; figures moving beyond it—animal figures ...reptilian. And then ...an eye is revealed.*

PRECEDING PAGES AND OPPOSITE: *Visual development art by Karen De Jong.*

BELOW: *Storyboard art by Ralph Zondag.*

dozen years ago, it was something that everyone here at Disney immediately saw the possibilities in," Michael Eisner, CEO and Chairman of The Walt Disney Company, recalls. "I like dinosaurs. I like the whole idea. I like the historical and scientific drama of it. Living dinosaurs gave us both exciting visual opportunities and unusual story possibilities."

Although it's hard to conceive now, this simple but novel thought seemed, at the time, about as *au courant* as mounting an operetta. Disney first expressed enthusiasm for this concept in 1987, at a time when "dinosaur movies" were cheesy cinematic relics—scientifically inaccurate stories with crude special effects (usually involving lizards with makeup shot in slow motion, or actors in dinosaur suits). Some of these dinosaur films were fine, some abysmal, none of them terribly credible.

Disney's *Dinosaur* has undergone a lengthy and unusual evolution. Something in the basic concept of the film captured the imagination and passion of a variety of people throughout the Disney organization. Although it would take more than a decade to reach the screen, the strength of its first central idea managed to make this arduous journey intact.

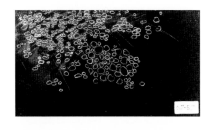

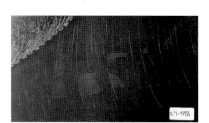

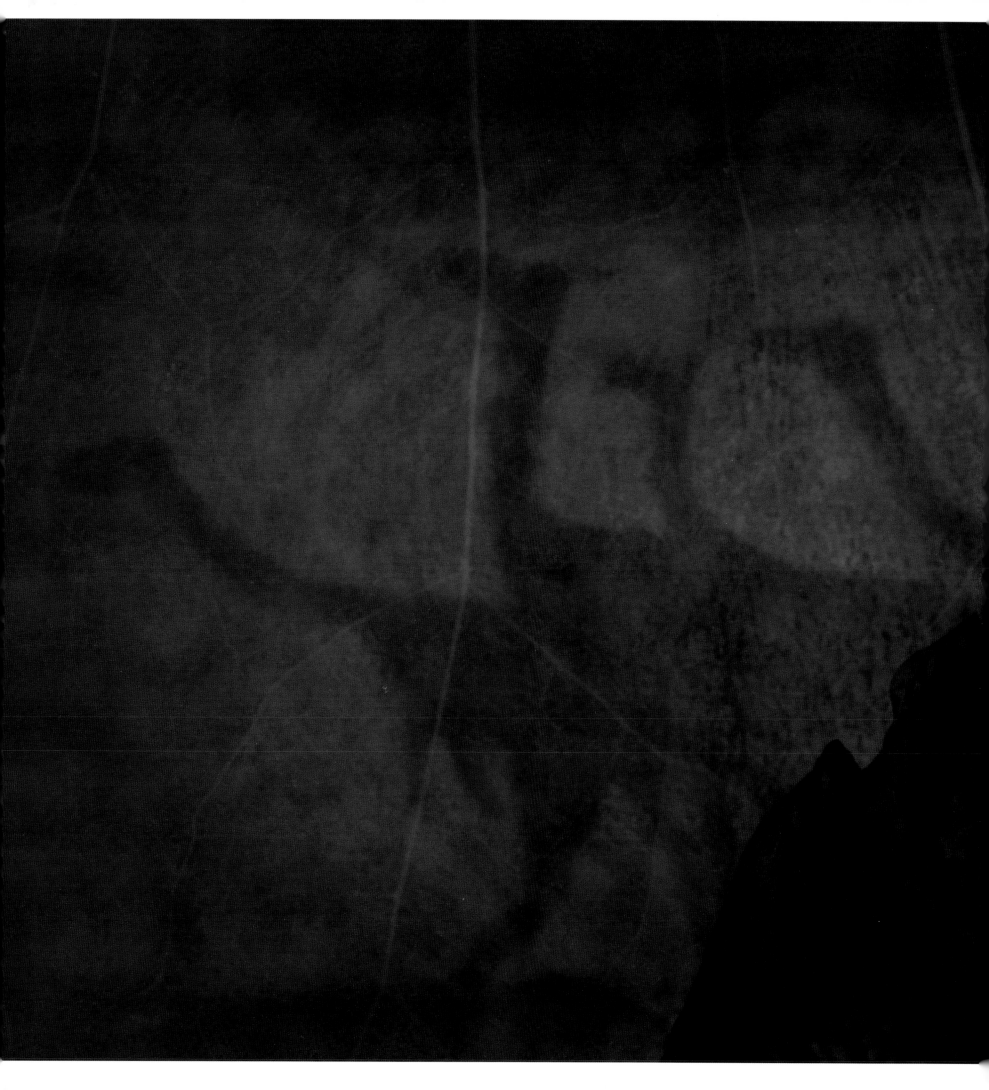

THE BIG BANG

The evolution of *Dinosaur* began with special-effects maven Phil Tippett and action director Paul Verhoeven. On the set of *RoboCop* (1987), Tippett engaged Verhoeven in a discussion about his concept for a "dinosaur movie" he'd been toying with, one that would portray a Cretaceous world in a photorealistic vérité style à la *National Geographic* about dinosaurs. Excited by the "big bang" of this idea, Verhoeven, Tippett, and producer Jon Davison pitched the idea to The Walt Disney Studios, where it was enthusiastically received and put into development through the studio's live-action film division.

The studio originally envisioned the film as the most elaborate stop-motion project ever mounted. Using dimensional objects repositioned one frame at a time to create the illusion of motion, stop-motion has been an animation technique for decades, from *King Kong* (1933) to Tim Burton's *The Nightmare Before Christmas* (1993).

Verhoeven and Tippett engaged writer/director/producer Walon Green to develop a story treatment for the project. The screenwriter of such films as *The Wild Bunch* (1969) and *Sorcerer* (1977), Green had also directed *The Secret Life of Plants* (1978) and several *National Geographic* documentaries for television in the 1960s. Green's experience proved a perfect mix for the style that Tippett and Verhoeven imagined for the "dinosaur movie."

THE SOUND OF SILENCE

Verhoeven and Tippett's idea was to make a silent film. "It would be an experiential sort of trip into the Cretaceous world, with a simple story about dinosaurs that people could follow and relate to without dialogue," recalls Green. "They thought it was challenging and daring, something different. I wrote a pretty extensive treatment, which we were going to use instead of a script. Since there was no dialogue, we were going to storyboard from the treatment.

"The whole thing was a pretty revolutionary idea," Green continues. "We looked at *Bambi* (1942) and *The Bear* (1989), and we thought, you know, for 84 minutes, this could work."

FISCAL ALERT

Once Green completed his treatment, the finance department went to work, too. Preliminary budgets began to surface—and warning signals began to flare. "They wanted to make the whole movie for around $20 million," then–Disney production chief Marty Katz told *The Hollywood Reporter* in 1999. But the budget came in at more than triple the amount—a whopping $72 million.

Again, though, the concept reigned. Everyone liked this dinosaur idea, and many executives felt that with a little creative thinking, there was still a way to get this dinosaur movie off the ground. Then, on November 9, 1989, the Berlin Wall came crumbling down, and previously untouchable locales in Eastern Europe opened up to the West. Within these regions, an abundance of animation talent lay untapped.

DINOSAURS RANGED FROM THE SIZE OF A CHICKEN (*COMPSOGNATHUS LONGIPES*) TO THE 14-METER, 7-METRIC TON *GIGANTOSAURUS CAROLINII*.

Dinosaur Pop

Since the term "dinosaur" entered our nomenclature more than a century and a half ago, the beasts have occupied a conspicuous space in popular culture, in novels from Sir Arthur Conan Doyle's *The Lost World* (1912)

to Eric Garcia's *Anonymous Rex* (1999); in films from *Gertie the Dinosaur* (1914) to *Jurassic Park: The Lost World* (1997); on television in programs both fictional (*Land of the Lost*, *Dinosaurs*) and documentary (*When Dinosaurs Ruled*, *Dinosaur!*); in comic books and graphic novels (*Alley Oop*, *Cadillacs & Dinosaurs*); supermarket tabloids; clothing and accessories; and even food products.

And toys. Oh, heavens, the toys. Dinosaur dolls, models, inflatables, games—even snow domes and house slippers—are a staple of toy stores and hobby shops around the world. What's the deal with this seemingly constant cultural fascination with the "terrible lizards"? Thomas Schumacher, president of Walt Disney Feature Animation, says, "When you're a kid, you're small, and without power, or advocacy, or voice. Then you learn about a great big monster, a mythical dragon—but it was real and it lived. Maybe even right in your own hometown they've

found fossils. That's a very cool idea, especially when you're a kid. You can become a dinosaur and chew up your tormentors."

As the dinosaur-loving kid grows older, this childhood fascination can lead to a scholarly lifelong interest, or take on a nostalgia of youth and innocence—which often leads to a winsome, sometimes syrupy revisitation of dinosaur iconography. "Dinosaurs have edged out flamingos as icons of kitsch," Stephen Jay Gould observed in *Natural History Magazine*. "I even saw dinosaur toilet paper with a different creature on each perforated segment."

"The dinosaur endures," according to author W. J. T. Mitchell, "because it is uniquely malleable, a figure of both innovation and obsolescence, massive power and pathetic failure—the totem animal of modernity."

BELOW: *The carnotaurs from* Dinosaur.

A TRIBUTE TO THE ONGOING HUMAN FASCINATION WITH DINOSAURS IS THE FACT THAT FROM ITS

Movie Dinosaurs

INFANCY, THE MOTION PICTURE MEDIUM HAS BEEN USED TO PORTRAY

DINOSAURS—WITH WILDLY VARYING SUCCESS. SEE IF YOU CAN

MATCH SOME OF THE MORE NOTABLE CELLULOID DINOSAUR MOVIE TITLES WITH THEIR DESCRIPTIONS:

1. A milestone in animation history, Winsor McCay incorporated this film's prehistoric title character into a popular vaudeville act by acting as an onstage "trainer" to the animated dino.

2. The legendary stop-motion animator Willis O'Brien produced this and a number of other short stop-motion dinosaur films, including *The Ghost of Slumber Mountain*, *Morpheus Mike*, *Prehistoric Poultry*, *Curious Pets of Our Ancestors*, and *R.F.D. 10000 B.C.* in 1917 for Thomas Edison Studio.

3. Based upon the 1912 novel by Sir Arthur Conan Doyle, this film's state-of-the-art special effects and stop-motion animation were the work of Willis H. O'Brien, who would later bring *King Kong* to life.

4. Produced by the Fleischer Studios in Miami, Florida, this animated short series was almost certainly one of the inspirations for the 1960-1966 *The Flintstones* TV series.

5. The original version of this film released in Japan in 1954 as *Gojira*. The title character became an atomic anti-hero in Japan. In subsequent films—and there were many—he evolved into a national superhero. The dinosaur effects essentially involve a guy in a hybrid dinosaur suit and detailed miniature sets that get stomped on.

6. Handsome wide-screen adventure/fantasy adapted from Jules Verne's novel. There are dozens of fanciful settings beneath the earth's surface, inhabited by weird humanoids and dinosaurs played by dressed-up monitor lizards. Remade in Spain as *Where Time Began* (1978) and for television in 1999.

7. The '70s equivalent of a 1940s movie serial, this low-budget British-made adventure is based on Edgar Rice Burroughs' (of Tarzan® fame) novel. Cheesy special effects (puppets and people dressed in dinosaur costumes among them). There was a similar sequel in 1977, called *The People That Time Forgot*.

8. Idiotic caveman comedy featuring Ringo Starr as an outcast in *One Zillion B.C.*, only watchable for Jim Danforth and David Allen's excellent dinosaur effects (which are also funnier than the human cast). Unless Ringo was your favorite Beatle.

9. Low-budget king Roger Corman released this *Jurassic Park*™ knock-off within months of Spielberg's epic. Corman impertinently cast Diane Ladd (mother of *Jurassic Park*™ star Laura Dern) in the lead. British pulp writer Harry Adam Knight provided the story. The dinosaurs are clumsy animatronic puppets, but you have to admire the chutzpah of the whole venture.

10. A billionaire constructs an island amusement park populated with real dinosaurs, created by genetic engineering and so well-conceived that nothing can possibly go wrong. Derivative, formulaic, predictable, and a whole lot of theme park-style summer movie fun—with special effects that rewrote the rule books and won an Oscar.

11. Four dinosaurs visit modern-day Manhattan in this animated feature directed by a couple of guys named Dick Zondag and Ralph Zondag, executive-produced by Steven Spielberg, and released the same year he made some other dinosaur movie.

A. *We're Back! A Dinosaur's Story* (1993)

B. *Journey to the Center of the Earth* (1959)

C. *Jurassic Park*™ (1993)

D. *Godzilla* (1998)

E. *The Land That Time Forgot* (1975)

F. *Caveman* (1981)

G. *Carnosaur* (1993)

H. *Gertie the Dinosaur (1914)* aka *Gertie the Trained Dinosaur*)

I. *The Lost World* (1925)

J. *Godzilla, King of the Monsters* (1956)

K. *The Dinosaur and the Missing Link* (1917)

L. *Stone Age Cartoons* (1940)

ANIMATION IN EASTERN EUROPE?

Schumacher remembers, "In 1990, I had just finished *The Rescuers Down Under*, and that December I was asked to travel to Eastern Europe to set up a program to bring animators to the U.S., train them, have them work with us as an exchange, and then send them back to their countries. So I went to Prague, Moscow, Budapest, and Zagreb, meeting with people and looking for animators and trying to help set up this program.

"The reason my contact over there knew a lot of different animation studios was because he had already done a trip, looking for stop-motion animators and animation studios. So while I traveled around Eastern Europe looking for my traditional animators, I was meeting with people who had also been talked with about the stop-motion animation to make this dinosaur film."

HOW DO WE MAKE THIS MOVIE?

During the period of the Eastern European research, the Disney filmmakers began to examine the idea of combining animatronics, live-action, and stop-motion technologies as a way to get the film made.

Meanwhile, in Berkeley, Phil Tippett, supervised a successful stop-motion test at his studio.

"All this stuff sort of weaves in," Schumacher says, "because shortly afterward, the Phil Tippett Studio was the facility that we rented to do the stop-motion tests for Tim Burton's *The Nightmare Before Christmas*. And then, after all this talk about stop-motion on *Dinosaur*, we wound up making a stop-motion movie with Tim Burton and Henry Selick, *The Nightmare Before Christmas*—never actually having made a movie with Phil Tippett."

A shift in thinking occurred about the story-telling convention of the film. Green remembers, "They came back and said, 'I know you don't want to have these animals speaking, but would you do a voice-over version, where the story is the same visual story, but the little mammal is telling the story?' So I did a version like that, and I thought, 'I don't know if this'll work or not.'"

THE EARLIEST KNOWN DESCRIPTION OF DINOSAUR BONES COMES FROM CHINESE APOTHECARIES (NEARLY 3000 B.C.). THOUGHT TO BE DRAGON BONES, THESE ARTIFACTS WERE (AND ARE STILL) CRUSHED FOR USE IN MEDICINES.

SUSPENDED ANIMATION

Then the unexpected happened. Phil Tippett hit the creative brakes. After seeing numerous tests and demonstrations in computer animation advancements, his concept of a stop-motion dinosaur film began to lose its luster. Tippett finally conceded that stop-motion wasn't right for this movie. By the time the dinosaur project would be completed, it would look quaint in comparison to the Computer Generated Imagery (CGI) that was quickly developing all around it, rather than stunning and revolutionary.

However, CGI technology was still prehistoric, insofar as being able to support an entire film. So, *Dinosaur* fell into the nebulous space between filmmaking technologies—one too archaic to achieve the photorealism the filmmakers desired, and one too undeveloped to carry it off.

"The path of this film was difficult to bring into focus," recalls Schumacher. "No one quite knew how to bring it to life. Could we make it over in Feature Animation? In 1990, the answer was 'no.' We simply didn't do character animation on computers back then. So the idea went fallow." The dinosaur movie entered a netherworld that film executives call "Development Hell," where it curled up and went dormant.

At least for a while.

PART TWO COUNTDOWN TO EXTINCTION: FINDING A FILM

FAILURES BEGETS SUCCESS

Several works that are considered part of the Disney Classic canon actually had rather rocky beginnings. Both *Peter Pan* (1953) and *Alice in Wonderland* (1951) began development at the time of the release of *Snow White and the Seven Dwarfs* (1937). Two fairy tales, *The Little Mermaid* and *The Steadfast Tin Soldier*, were developed in the late 1930s as part of an ambitious Hans Christian Andersen film biography that Walt Disney envisioned in collaboration with production mogul Samuel Goldwyn. *The Little Mermaid* finally surfaced in 1989 as an animated feature, *The Steadfast Tin Soldier* as a segment in *Fantasia/2000*. The entire Disney creative culture exists with an awareness that wonderfully imaginative ideas get shelved—and often are resurrected years later.

"Good ideas never go away," says Walt Disney Imagineering vice chairman and principal creative executive Marty Sklar. "They are a precious commodity, whether developed right away or not. A good idea is never forgotten. It may turn up sometime later for use in some other project, in part, or in its entirety."

> "Sometimes you gotta create what you want to be a part of." —Geri Weitzman

Dinosaur was no exception. Sklar's comment couldn't be more appropriate, since the creative spark plug that jolted the dinosaur movie out of its dormancy turned out to be a Walt Disney Imagineering project.

COUNTDOWN TO EXTINCTION

In 1993, Walt Disney Imagineering (WDI) was immersed in a new theme park for Walt Disney World, Disney's Animal Kingdom. The Imagineers were designing themed areas and attractions in anticipation of a 1996 opening date.

"When the company started Disney's Animal Kingdom," recalls Schumacher, "there was an area called DinoLand, and the Imagineers wanted to build a dinosaur attraction with a ride. Michael [Eisner] said, 'Let's bring back that dinosaur idea.' Developing the film along with an attraction would create a kind of reciprocal process between The Studio and WDI."

PRECEDING PAGES: *Ominous clouds approach from the sea as meteors of fire mercilessly rain down on Lemur Island. Production still.*

TYRANNOSAURUS REX ("TYRANT LIZARD") WAS NEITHER THE BIGGEST NOR THE MOST FEROCIOUS OF THE DINOSAURS, BUT HE IS STILL POPULAR CULTURE'S FAVORITE.

"It just always makes sense, wherever possible, to link our film entertainment and our three-dimensional entertainment efforts," Eisner states. "Whether *It's Tough to Be a Bug* features characters from *A Bug's Life* in Disney's Animal Kingdom, or *Dick Tracy* appears at Disney-MGM Studios, our audiences enjoy and expect the connection of filmed and theme-park entertainments."

Schumacher continues, "So Michael wanted to make this movie, but we didn't have a story. All we knew is that it had to have dinosaurs, and at the time it was called *Countdown to Extinction*, like the attraction at Animal Kingdom."

THIS PAGE: *Carnotaurs at DinoLand, Animal Kingdom.*

A PUZZLE MADE OF ASHES

"So we tried to come up with a few new ideas," Schumacher sighs. "It seemed like practically everybody in Hollywood had tried their hand at it by now—there were piles of treatments and scripts. But toward the end of 1994, Michael was really eager, saying, 'I want to make this dinosaur movie.'"

Schumacher and his colleagues began to put the *Dinosaur* pieces together. But they faced a large problem. No one seriously considered executing the film by any other method than computer animation, and since the initial work on the film, computer animation had made extraordinary leaps, in both live action and animation.

23

TOYING WITH THE COMPUTER

In the interest of increasing the rate at which they released animated movies, Walt Disney Feature Animation experimented with other forms of animation. The Pixar Animation Studios team, with a series of award-winning computer-animated shorts and several outstanding computer-animated television commercials behind them, felt ready to take the first steps toward a long-cherished goal of making a feature-length, computer-animated film, and the two studios entered into another collaboration.

The result was *Toy Story,* a gigantically complicated application of the latest computer technology, used to tell the story of a group of children's toys whose world is the suburban bedroom of a little boy. "Although *Toy Story* became the highest-grossing family film of 1995, and the top-selling video release of 1996, and even won an Oscar for Special Achievement, the time we're talking about is pre-*Toy Story,*" reminds Schumacher. "I don't know if we had the adamant confidence then that we do now.

"We also didn't want to appear to be setting up a Disney department that 'did what Pixar does,'" Schumacher continues, "primarily because we wouldn't spend a lot of effort on anything so utterly impossible. It would be like trying to deny physics. John Lasseter and his crew are simply geniuses, and so unparalleled at what they do, that trying to ape them would have been an exercise in foolishness.

"We realized that Pixar's style has an idiom all it's own. They've created a visual vernacular all their own. Our whole point with *Dinosaur* was to make the dinosaurs absolutely *real.*"

WHAT ABOUT ILM?

When Kathleen Gavin, senior vice president of production for Walt Disney Feature Animation, first started on the project, she and others kicked around the idea of hiring International Light and Magic (ILM), George Lucas's cutting-edge special-effects house, to do the job.

"Then it occurred to us that ILM simply wasn't going to shut down their very successful business while they took on this one project," says Gavin. "In order to accommodate *Dinosaur,* ILM would have had to go build another arm of its studio, hire more people, buy more equipment, the whole thing. Can you imagine how much that would cost? Way too much for the budget of a single film. If we're essentially spending that money to build a facility, wouldn't it be better for us to build a facility that is part of Disney?"

CAPS

Walt Disney Feature Animation entered the computer age in 1986, when Disney and Pixar Animation Studios started a joint technical development called CAPS (Computer Animated Production System). The CAPS system allowed the hand-drawn inking and painting process to be done on the computer. Instead of artists using brushes, they could now use an electronic color palette to create finished "paintings." Disney first experimented with CAPS for one scene in *The Little Mermaid* (1989), and has since gone on to use and develop the system on all of its subsequent animated features.

For many years, a group of Disney animators and Imagineers gathered together weekly, at either Alphonse's Restaurant in Toluca Lake or Walt Disney's personal favorite, the Tam O'Shanter on Los Feliz Boulevard, to eat, drink, critique, gripe, catch up, and reminisce. Disney legend Ken Anderson started the group, and anyone available on Thursdays would get together.

"I am not quite sure when these gatherings started," Disney animator Andreas Deja says, "but they welcomed younger artists, and I joined the group occasionally for a little 'martini lunch.'" Other Disney artists who dropped in reveled in the recollections, anecdotes, and opinions—a living archive of the art and legacy of Disney. "It was a lot of fun," Deja recalls. "I had the chance to meet and hang out with people like Ken Anderson, Claude Coats, Bill Layne, Marc Davis, and occasionally Frank Thomas and Ollie Johnston."

Sadly, these luncheons stopped with the passing of Ken Anderson in 1993.

And the nickname for this gathering: "The Dinosaur Club."

DEVELOPING TECHNOLOGY

By continually developing new technology for its animated films, Walt Disney Feature Animation was actually a big part of the boom in CGI/digital animation. Every feature has inspired the creation of new animation methods, many of them computer-based.

"There's also been a focus here to avoid building 'one-offs,'" says Gavin. That is to say, Disney has been conscientious about developing technology rather than create a tool that is used once to accomplish something specific, and then forgotten.

"So with our desire to focus our developing technology systems in one place and apply them to future projects," continues Gavin, "and our desire to create this film with realistic dinosaurs, it became obvious that there actually was a real need at Disney to have a digital studio. This group could support

our live-action movies, television, our CG movies, animation, projects with WDI, or anyone within the company who needs to have that kind of digital technology. Wouldn't it be better for the company to invest in that, and have *Dinosaur* be the first movie through it? Build a studio not just for one movie, but build a digital studio for the entire Disney company? That way, a movie like *Dinosaur* isn't bearing the cost of this huge factory; the factory will survive the film and be used for many years on many projects throughout the company."

"*Dinosaur* became a movie we were making for two reasons," Schumacher explains. "First, it tied in to the Animal Kingdom project, and second, because it would break new ground in technology, we could justify building our own digital facility. Then we'd have our own special effects house for The Walt Disney Company."

EORAPTOR LUNENSIS ("DAWN PLUNDERER") IS THE EARLIEST KNOWN DINOSAUR, BELIEVED TO HAVE LIVED 227,000,000 YEARS AGO.

ABOVE: *One of the menacing raptors from* Dinosaur.

25

THE WALT DISNEY COMPANY HASN'T EXACTLY TRAILED THE HERD IN THE CREATION OF "DINOSAUR POP." DINOSAURS HAVE MADE FREQUENT APPEARANCES IN THE WONDERFUL WORLD OF DISNEY:

"THE RITE OF SPRING" FROM *FANTASIA* (1940)

The thirty-minute visualization of Igor Stravinsky's "Le Sacre du Printemps" was the centerpiece of Disney's *Fantasia*, and featured nothing less than the story of the evolution of life on Earth. "From the outset," animator John Hubley recalled, "*Rite of Spring* was conceived as a scientific document." Walt Disney himself explained that his intent with the piece was to make it seem "as though the studio had sent an expedition back to the earth six million years ago." So vivid and powerful was Disney's portrayal of prehistoric life, that it had a lengthy afterlife as an educational film.

ONE OF OUR DINOSAURS IS MISSING (1975)

An unpretentious caper comedy based on the book *The Great Dinosaur Robbery* by David Forrest (David Eliades and Bob Forrest Webb), *One of Our Dinosaurs Is Missing* has an impressive cast including Helen Hayes, Peter Ustinov, and Clive Revill. It is actually only marginally concerned with the titular  dinosaur; rather, it is a spy-movie parody involving the pursuit of microfilm hidden in a dinosaur skeleton in a London museum. Art director Michael Stringer supervised six modelers in the construction of two 75-foot replica dinosaur skeletons, each weighing several tons.

BABY . . . SECRET OF THE LOST LEGEND (1985)

This film began life as a Disney movie but was ultimately released under the Touchstone Pictures banner. It came into being at a transitional point in the Studio's creative life, and uncomfortably straddles the family and adult film categories, while succeeding in neither. It calls to mind clichéd jungle adventure B movies while striving for touches of *Raiders of the Lost Ark*—which it misses.

The Seattle Times' John Hartl reasoned that "It's likely to be remembered as a $16 million mistake." Ah, for the days when $16 million was a lot of money in Hollywood.

MY SCIENCE PROJECT (1985)

A pair of teenagers must put together a science project in order to pass science class and graduate from high school. In a U.S. Air Force supply dump, they find a gadget that can cause a space-time warp. During their adventures with the time-traveling device, they encounter gladiators, a Neanderthal man, an Egyptian queen, and—hello, hello—a Tyrannosaurus rex. The dinosaur in *My Science Project* was a complex puppet, built and animated by Doug Beswick Productions, Inc. The film is essentially a series of effects, miniature, and animation gags.

"MONSTERS OF THE DEEP" ("DISNEYLAND" TV PROGRAM, 1955)

Aired on January 19, 1955, this episode of the Walt Disney-hosted anthology program featured a presentation on monsters—historic, scientific, mythical, and cinematic. It was what might today be termed something of a "clip

ABOVE: *Production still from* The Rite of Spring.

LEFT: *Production still from* One of Our Dinosaurs Is Missing.

show," since much of the featured content was derived from films like the *True-Life Adventures*, *20,000 Leagues Under the Sea* (1954) and the dinosaur segments of "The Rite of Spring" segment from *Fantasia*.

"DINOSAURS" (TV SERIES)

Created by Jim Henson Associates, "Dinosaurs" first aired on April 26, 1991 on ABC-TV. It was described as "a pre-hysterical comedy," and revolved around the daily lives of the Sinclairs (the old Sinclair Oil Company logo was a dinosaur), a highly-evolved anthropomorphized and domesticated dinosaur family, providing a comedic look at our contemporary society in the process.

Although popular, critically well-regarded, and Emmy-winning, "Dinosaurs" had its last airing on July 20, 1994. It has gone on to steady popularity in syndication and on the Disney Channel.

TWO TRACKS

"Now it made sense," Gavin says. "It really, truly, finally made sense to do the movie. There had been so many advances digitally to really do it. Now our job was to start putting teams of people together that came from very disparate backgrounds, creative and technical."

> "The first rule to tinkering is to save all the parts." —Paul Erlich

The real making of *Dinosaur* finally began concurrent with the creation of Disney's Digital Studio. Thus a massive renovation of a vacant Lockheed building across from the Burbank Airport. Disney gutted the 200,000-square-foot, four-story building, then completely redesigned and tailored it to the requirements of computer-based digital animation. The creative team was primarily comprised of artists working in this new building in Burbank, who gained support from a small but effective team based out of the Florida animation studio.

RIGHT: *Feature Animaton's Northside facility in Burbank.*

BOTTOM LEFT: *Guests at DinoLand USA observe the preparations of a tyrannosaur skeleton, named Sue.*

RIGHT: *A chart marking "Sue's" progress.*

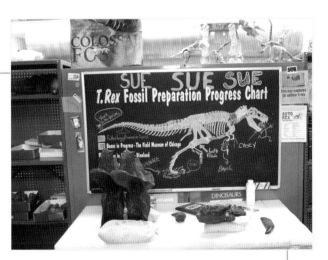

The Fifty-Nine-Foot Tyrannosaur

A rare tyrannosaur has been residing at Disney's Animal Kingdom while it undergoes scientific preparatory work.

Discovered in 1990, it is the most complete skeleton of a T-rex ever found. The full skeleton will go on permanent display at The Field Museum in Chicago this year.

Guests in DinoLand USA (part of Disney's Animal Kingdom) have watched Field staffers conduct the painstaking work of preparing the dinosaur for display.

Once the originals are returned to Chicago, a life-sized replica of the bones eventually will be on permanent display at Disney's Animal Kingdom.

The 59-foot-long tyrannosaur, nicknamed Sue, was acquired by Field at an auction on October 4, 1997. Field was supported in its winning bid by Walt Disney World Resort®, McDonald's Corp.®, and the California State University System.

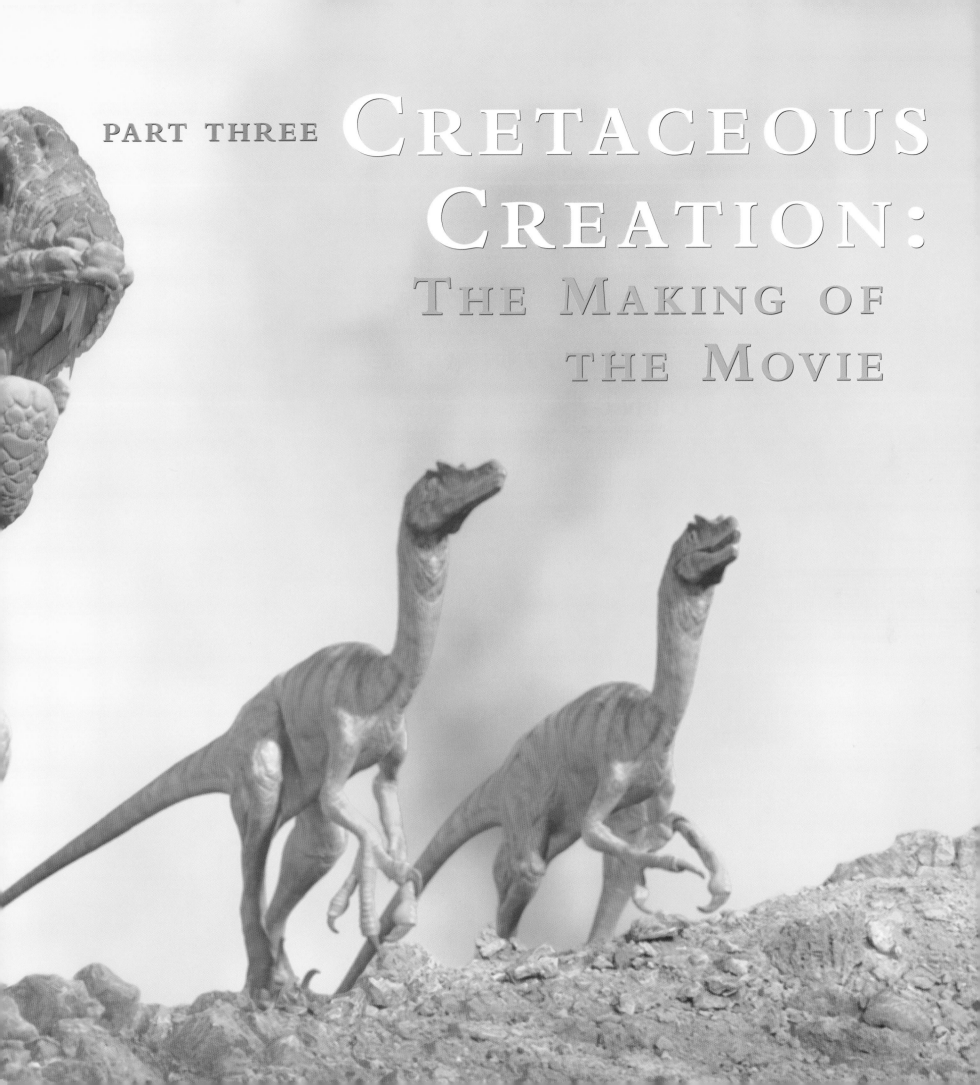

PART THREE **CRETACEOUS CREATION:** THE MAKING OF THE MOVIE

TEAM BUILDING

Although rarely emphasized, one of the most vital aspects of filmmaking is the creative production team that will see a project through from inception to completion. Assembling such a team is a delicate process, and this exacting balance of skills and personalities is as important as any other part of filmmaking.

"Any sufficiently advanced technology is indistinguishable from magic." —Arthur C. Clarke, *Technology and the Future*

"THEATER PEOPLE"

Many of the key figures at Walt Disney Feature Animation have backgrounds in live theater. "I think one of the reasons Tom and Peter always hire theater people is because we are hungry for knowledge," *Dinosaur* producer Pam Marsden says. "Typically we like learning new things. I also think that we tend to throw ourselves at projects without a net, because there's a sense of commitment.

"Theater people tend to know very well how to orchestrate a group of egos," Marsden continues. "We're very artist-friendly, which is important when you're dealing in an artistic medium. We acknowledge the needs of artistry. I think that we allow space and time, and it's really okay if you don't do it inside the lines, between nine and five."

A SIX MONTH GIG?: PAM MARSDEN

While serving as the resident production stage manager of Chicago's St. Nicholas Theatre, Marsden worked with a managing director named Peter Schneider. In 1984, she worked on the Olympic Arts Festival in Los Angeles with Schneider and a fellow named Thomas Schumacher.

"Peter Schneider and I had both worked with Pam in Chicago," Kathleen Gavin says. "We'd offered her jobs numerous times, and she'd turned us down, but she finally was at a place in her life where she thought maybe she should try this. We had this test for *Dinosaur*, and sort of lured her here with the promise of doing a six-month test."

"It's kind of fun to do the impossible." —Walt Disney

30

"I didn't want to live in Los Angeles," Marsden recalls. "I had a nice job in Chicago as the Managing Director of the International Theater Festival of Chicago. I love the Midwest and I'm very much a midwestern girl. So I maneuvered to leave my kids and husband for three months. At the three-month point, I *knew* that we weren't going to finish in another three months. So my family moved out here, and about a year into it, I finally realized that this wasn't 'a six-month gig'—it was a full-time thing. It had turned into a movie. At that point I decided to sign a contract and stay on."

Mulan producer Pam Coats, who now serves as senior vice president of creative affairs for Walt Disney Feature Animation, remembers a similar situation, "Tom and Peter are very good at getting you in here and getting you involved. I was supposed to squire *Mulan* (1998) through a transitional production period and then go away. By the time that happened, though, I was so in love with the film and with my team, that I didn't want to leave. I think Pam Marsden had the same experience. By the time the test was done, she just didn't want to leave."

BELOW: *Scenes from the animation test.*

FROM THE BEGINNING: RALPH ZONDAG

Ralph Zondag's previous experience with animation, directing, and dinosaurs made him a perfect match for the film. Most notably he directed *We're Back: A Dinosaur's Story* (1993). In addition, Zondag's credits include a veritable laundry list of many of the best-known non-Disney animated features of the last fifteen years; *An American Tail* (1986), *All Dogs Go to Heaven* (1989), *Rock-A-Doodle* (1992), *Thumbelina* (1994), and *A Troll in Central Park* (1994) among them. "I had wanted to work at Disney since high school, though," Zondag admits.

"I came over to Disney to work on *Pocahontas* on story," Zondag explains. "I have an animation background, but I really wanted to take in directing. Walt Disney Feature Animation is so geared to getting those storyboards up and working—so I really wanted to put all my attention to the boarding, getting the story reels up, all that sort of thing. So that's the role I focused on with *Pocahontas*.

"That paved the way for me to have the opportunity to direct *Dinosaur*," Zondag says. "I started here literally from the beginning—it started out just as a little one-minute test, which I was brought on to codirect.

"For the test, we worked with miniature sets, and we were trying to establish both a 'look' and a 'feel' for the film," Zondag continues. "We developed a couple of characters, and how they would move, and speak, and what have you. First and

ALADAR: **I WAS TALKIN' TO THEM, AND I GUESS THEY'RE HAVING A HARD TIME KEEPING UP . . .**

ALADAR: **. . . SO, YOU KNOW, MAYBE YOU COULD SLOW IT DOWN A BIT.**

KRON: **LET THE WEAK SET THE PACE . . . NOW THERE'S AN IDEA.**

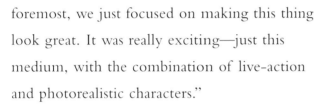

THIS PAGE: *Storyboard art by Ralph Zondag.*

KRON: **BETTER LET ME DO THE THINKING FROM NOW ON, ALADAR.**

foremost, we just focused on making this thing look great. It was really exciting—just this medium, with the combination of live-action and photorealistic characters."

Zondag also employed his formidable design talents. He, along with codirector Leighton, contributed extensively to, and closely supervised, all of the film's character design work. "When you have characters as realistic as these are," states Zondag, "you can't get too exaggerated. The emotions have to play very real. We had to find a way to style the characters so they would play as real as any character of a live-action picture."

After the completion of the test, Zondag faced a choice. "The film really wasn't even green-lit yet, and I had the opportunity to go and direct another feature," he explains. "I decided I'd rather risk it and do this. It was more exciting—brand-new. So I just chose to stay on here. I've never regretted my choice."

A NUTS-AND-BOLTS GUY: ERIC LEIGHTON

Eric Leighton, a veteran of stop-motion animation, has worked on dozens of projects for Colossal Pictures, ILM, Tippett Studios, and Henry Selick Productions. Leighton's work has been seen in television commercials and promos, the *Gumby* TV series, *Robocop II,* and the Academy Award®-nominated film for best visual effects, Tim Burton's *The Nightmare Before Christmas.*

Leighton started with *Dinosaur* back in the early days. "The first time I read a script for this movie was in 1988," Leighton recalls. "Walon Green's script was pitched to me by Phil Tippett when he planned to execute it in stop-motion."

ABOVE: *Art from the* Dinosaur *test phase by Thom Enriquez.*

Years later, when Kathleen Gavin approached Leighton again with *Dinosaur*—this time as a CGI feature—he had an immediate and strong response: "I'm always interested in naturalistic movement and creating things in animation that you can do in no other place. And dinosaurs were obviously the perfect character choice for that kind of thing."

Gavin initially assigned Leighton as an animation supervisor on *Dinosaur*. Leighton remained in that position for a couple of years until he was invited to step in as codirector.

"I personally am very much a nuts-and-bolts guy," Leighton explains. "I worked on *Nightmare* as animation supervisor for three and a half years and helped intensively to develop all methodology and process on that film. I did the same on *Dinosaur*, working especially on animation tool building and interface creation. We worked extensively on creating new or modifying existing software and hardware for the animators. Without this kind of 'preemptive strike' animating a show of this size would simply have not been feasible."

Leighton has enjoyed refining a technique and developing new frontiers and methodologies. "The ability to have the people and the backing to be able to push the craft as far as it can go is really an extraordinary opportunity for all of us here," he says. "Ultimately, what we're all here for is to experience as much as we can in life and learn new things. This is one heck of an opportunity to do that."

One more important element of *Dinosaur* attracted Leighton: "It had been a lifelong goal of mine to work at Disney," he admits. "In fact, when I was ten, I told my dad I wanted to be a Disney animator when I grew up. He told me I had plenty of time to change my mind. But I've always been a bit stubborn."

BAKER BLOODWORTH

Dinosaur coproducer Baker Bloodworth is another one of those "theater people" at Disney. A UCLA theater major, Bloodworth served at the Los Angeles Theatre Center and the Orange County Performing Arts Center. He was producer's assistant on Broadway productions of *Cabaret* and *Macbeth*, and company manager for the national touring company of *Cats* and the first Andrew Lloyd Webber Concert Tour (starring Sarah Brightman). His Disney credits include Florida unit production manager on *Beauty and the Beast* (1991) and *Aladdin* (1992), and associate producer on *Pocahontas* (1995).

Bloodworth had just finished *Pocahontas* when *Dinosaur* came his way. "I had been completely consumed by *Pocahontas*, and had gone off to sleep for four months. Then Tom and Peter came to me and said, 'We'd really like you to work on this movie called *Dinosaur*. We don't know what it's gonna be yet, but it's important to the company. Go take a look at it.'

"So I thought I'd just jump in and see if it worked," Bloodworth continues. "Fortunately, Pam and I were a great fit from the start. She's a great delegator and a great collaborator. When she welcomed me onto the project, I quickly realized that I didn't know a thing about the movie. I thought, 'Oh my God, this is a huge project! It's bigger than anything we've ever done on every level.' I got *really* excited about it and said, 'You know, this could be *fun*!'"

STARTING LINEUP

From the beginning, Paul Yanover shepherded *Dinosaur* as the vice president of technology for Walt Disney Feature Animation. Carolyn Soper and Tamara Boutcher were brought to the *Dinosaur* project as production managers. "Tamara understood animation already," Bloodworth explains. "Carolyn Soper, coming in from Buena Vista Visual Effects, understood the arena of live-action visual effects. Janet Healy from ILM was assigned as CG production specialist. Formerly with Warner Bros., Jinko Gotoh was brought on as manager of digital production. So we had the beginning of a really great team—our 'Gang of Six.'" Bloodworth continues, "Janet, Paul, and Jinko were the technology experts. Carolyn, Tamara and I were the Disney production experts. We formed the structure where all the ideas would be funneled to the 'gang.' We would then assess the recommendations and vote on how to proceed. If we didn't have a quorum, we would kick it up to Pam and Kathleen."

THREE HUGE SCARY THINGS

"The movie was off and running, and we were trying to gauge the scope of the project," Bloodworth recalls. "There were three huge scary things we had to do at that time, which no studio has ever done in such a short amount of time."

HUGE SCARY THING NUMBER ONE: SEARCHING FOR ARTISTS

"One, we had maybe forty artists by that point, and we needed, by our calculations, 350 of the world's greatest CG talent. This was at a time when the market was saturated with projects, and the artists had nothing but choices. So we put together a recruiting team with Leslie White, Pamela Focht, and Marjorie Randolph."

Their foremost challenge was to attract top professionals without pillaging the staffs of other companies. "How do you entice people to come to work on your film at Disney, which was not a sexy place for CG filmmaking?" continues Bloodworth. "We needed to create a 'cachet.' So we began with an egg—a very cool recruiting brochure with the image of a dinosaur egg."

The buzz they created worked. The rumor mills hummed of a very secret and ground-breaking Disney film that would be the pinnacle of its medium. No expense was to be spared on the project, since it would be the foundation of an ongoing state-of-the-art enterprise. "We hired 150 artists in the course of a year," Bloodworth says.

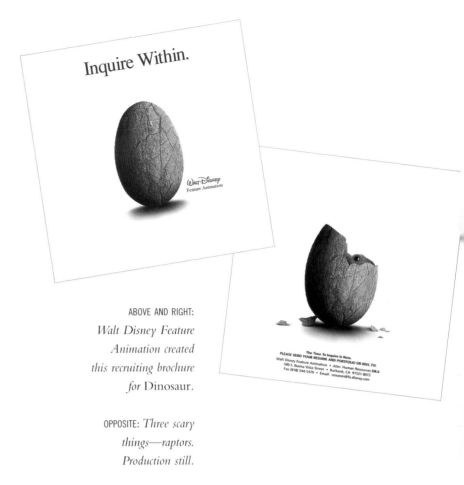

Inquire Within.

ABOVE AND RIGHT: *Walt Disney Feature Animation created this recruiting brochure for* Dinosaur.

OPPOSITE: *Three scary things—raptors. Production still.*

The issue of the *Dinosaur* expenses would continue to nag the production—even to the present. Rumors of

Money, Money, Money

a wildly careening budget have peppered press accounts of the project since the beginning, sometimes to the consternation (but usually to the amusement) of the executives. "What we're doing on *Dinosaur* is kind of . . . unexplainably groundbreaking," Schumacher explains. "It's hard to describe what we're doing, but everyone can understand money, so that's the hook they grab onto. We never talk about how much these projects cost, but sometimes on *Dinosaur* I wish we did, so people could share my amazement at what we've accomplished within reasonable financial parameters!

"Let me put it this way," Schumacher says. "I don't just work with the best artists, designers, and animators in the movie business. Our executives are equally as talented in logistics, accounting, and scheduling. And I'll leave it at that."

THE LARGEST DINOSAUR EGG YET FOUND IS ABOUT TEN INCHES LONG.

HUGE SCARY THING NUMBER TWO: "BUILDING THE MACHINE"

Bloodworth goes on, "By this time, we had this other group on another track trying to figure out how to 'build the machine.' On the first track, we still had the 'how do you make the movie?' team. Those two had to operate in tandem because how you make the movie dictates how you build the machine. Our machine has to last beyond *Dinosaur*—otherwise our investment is worth nothing."

These brainstorming discussions grew from the collective experiences and viewpoints of each of the department heads and leads as they were hired. Manager of digital production Jinko Gotoh, digital effects supervisor Neil Eskuri, visual effects supervisor Neil Krepela, effects lighting supervisor Chris Peterson, and effects compositing supervisor Jim Hillin all began the *Dinosaur* project by brainstorming about how they would make the film.

"Whoever it was that we brought into our team," Bloodworth says, "we asked, 'What is important to you? What is *not* important to you? How would *you* make this movie?' For six months we literally brainstormed every day."

As the "who" and "how" came together for *Dinosaur*, their new Northside Studio was nearing completion, and the components of "the machine" were beginning to materialize within

the building. Now, the team set out on their last and scariest track—to solidify the *Dinosaur* story.

HUGE SCARY THING NUMBER THREE: FINDING THE STORY

"With most of our projects, we begin with a story we'd like to tell," Schumacher explains. "This film didn't come to us that way. It came to us as a concept we wanted to try. Here's a thing we'd like to achieve, we want to have this technology to do it, we want to have it be like real dinosaurs. It's the first time we've done that."

Schumacher and his colleagues began looking at ways to integrate their technical and story objectives. "One of our goals is to keep telling our audience compelling stories that will give them a new view of themselves. Another goal is to keep inventing characters that you can identify with and that you'd like to meet again. But the important underlying pulse is the idea of breaking technological

ABOVE AND OPPOSITE TOP:
Aladar, with a "little" help from Baylene, discovers water under the dry lake bed. Storyboard art by Ralph Zondag.

OPPOSITE BOTTOM:
Production still.

38

ALADAR: **BAYLENE, DON'T MOVE**

ALADAR: **WAY TO GO, BAYLENE!**

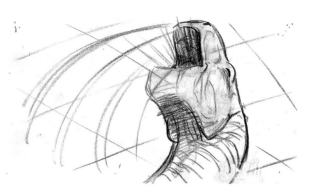

ALADAR: **(BELLOW!)**

barriers. Like Walt Disney himself, we always move forward, finding new things. But technology in and of itself has absolutely no artistic point of view."

DEATH AND EXTINCTION

Noted paleontologist John "Jack" Horner of Montana State University once said, "[Dinosaurs] were around for 140 million years, and we've only been here for 4 million. So you'd think we'd want to know why they were successful, instead of always concentrating on why they died."

The dinosaur's success became the essence of what Schumacher saw in the *Dinosaur* story. "A movie where all your heroes die at the end isn't too interesting to me. What *could* be significant in the story wasn't the portrayal of an event that causes immediate extinction, but showing how an environmental disaster dictates a change in the way the characters go on *living*. That became the small idea at the core of this movie."

ALADAR: **(GASP)**   ALADAR: **PLIO! YAR!**

ALADAR: **WHERE ARE YOU!?**   (O.S.) PLIO: **ALADAR!**   PLIO: **OVER HERE!**

STARTING UP THE STORY

Veteran art director and story man Thom Enriquez (*The Little Mermaid, The Lion King, Tummy Trouble*) led the story team. He began the process by ridding himself and his crew of the intimidation of the medium. "It wasn't any different than working on a 2-D animated feature. I think *every* movie we work on is a challenge. We are constantly pushing for different and more creative ideas. So we just went with the story we wanted to do, and didn't worry about the process. . . . We'd worry about that later."

ABOVE: *Fireballs from the heavens change the world of Aladar and his lemur friends forever. They are forced into the sea and must find a new way of life. Storyboard art by Thom Enriquez.*

LEFT AND OPPOSITE: *Production stills.*

13-722

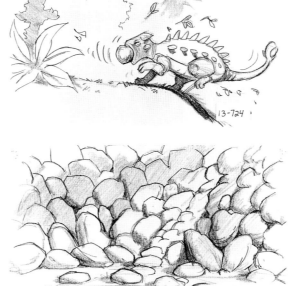

13-724

13-728

13-730

13-731

13-732

Sequences, Scenes, Storyboards, and Story Reels

An animated film doesn't begin as a script, but as a story divided into **sequences**. These sequences get drawn out as individual story sketches and placed sequentially on large bulletin boards. These **storyboards** look much like a comic strip, and serve to outline the action of the story. "Storyboards act as a blueprint for the filmmakers," Thom Enriquez explains, "defining the basic layout, action, and dialogue for each scene."

Within a sequence, each different section of animation is called a **scene**. The breakdown of sequences and scenes, along with a description of their corresponding action and dialogue, is compiled in the animation draft. "This draft really serves as a beginning 'script' for the production team," Enriquez says, "but it is by no means anything final. It's a work-in-progress document."

In order to evaluate how a particular section of the film plays, story sketches are edited together with temporary audio tracks of dialogue, music, and sound effects. These are known as **story reels**.

"Unlike live-action filmmaking, where the footage is shot from a finished script and then edited, animated features are developed through a process of trial and error with various ideas and concepts," editor H. Lee Peterson says. "Some sequences are tightened and refined, others are augmented, while some are replaced or completely abandoned."

This early development phase is the beginning of the editorial process. Rather than taking finished shots and beginning to assemble the film, Peterson and his team collaborate on the film's structure, pace, timing, and dialogue throughout the life of the production.

TOP: *Url finds the rockpile of his dreams. Storyboard art by Darryl Kidder.*

RIGHT: *Art from the* Dinosaur *test phase by Thom Enriquez.*

LEFT AND BELOW: *Storyboard art by Ray Shenusay.*

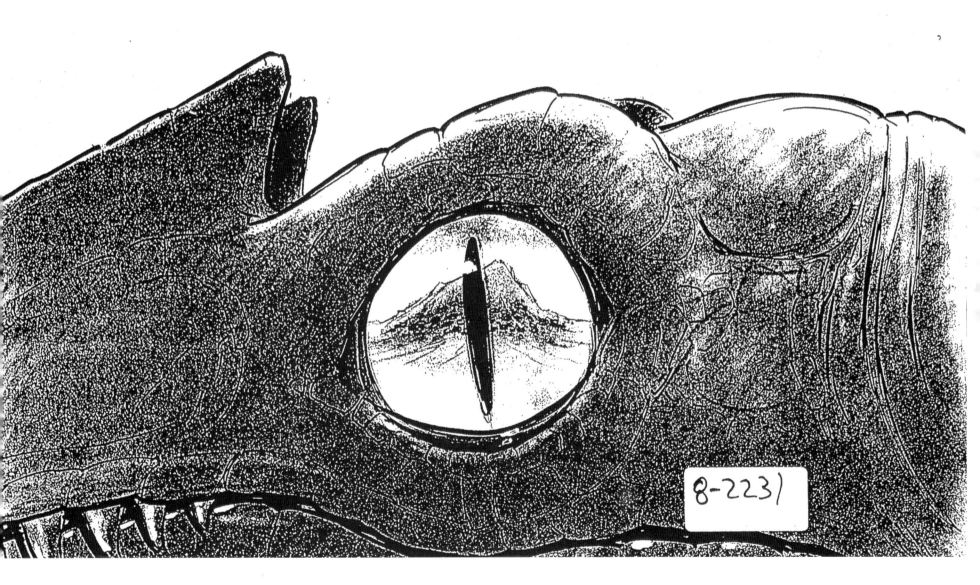

8-2231

LEFT: *Storyboard art by Dick Zondag.*

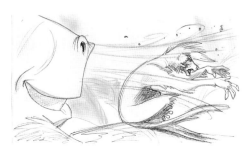

(O.S.) BRUTON: **WHY IS HE DOING THIS?**

BRUTON: **... PUSHING THEM ON WITH FALSE HOPE.**

PLIO: **IT'S HOPE THAT'S GOTTEN US THIS FAR.**

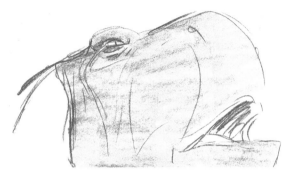

BRUTON: **BUT WHY DOESN'T HE LET THEM ACCEPT THEIR FATE?**

BRUTON: **I'VE ACCEPTED MINE.**

PLIO: **AND WHAT IS YOUR FATE?**

ABOVE AND LEFT:
Storyboard art by
Thom Enriquez.

BELOW AND BOTTOM LEFT:
Storyboard art by
Frank Nissen.

BRUTON: **TO DIE HERE ... IT'S THE WAY THINGS ARE.**

PLIO: **ONLY IF YOU GIVE UP, BRUTON. IT'S YOUR CHOICE,
NOT YOUR FATE.**

TO SPEAK OR NOT TO SPEAK

The initial vérité style of nonspeaking characters still needed to be addressed. One version proposed to have a lemur character narrate the story. Another version proposed voice-over. Schumacher recalls, "The proof-of-concept test was like *Homeward Bound: The Incredible Journey* (1993), where all the character voices were delivered in voice-over—mainly because we couldn't figure out how to make the characters talk while remaining believable."

Michael Eisner viewed a voice-over test and found the contrary to be true: "The characters conversing without mouth movement felt strange—and actually *emphasized* a technical inability to accomplish the sophisticated facial animation required for believable mouth movements."

Eisner's comment epitomized the struggle of numerous *Dinosaur* animators. The filmmakers had become concerned—perhaps too concerned—with a kind of absolute scientific factuality. By creating their own exacting boundaries of what constituted truth or inaccuracy, science or fantasy, they had taken the idea of "science" much too seriously. By doing so, the artists had created an air of taking creative license head-on.

BELIEVE IT OR NOT

The *Dinosaur* filmmakers regrouped, and after much discussion realized that what they sought to achieve was veracity. Not a scientific veracity, but a *believability*. "I look at it this way: everything we 'know' is just 'paleoconjecture,'" Thom Enriquez chuckles. "Well, we work at Disney. At Disney, the animals do talk. It's one of the things that Disney has always done really well. It's part of the magic of animation."

"In our hearts, we knew eventually they would speak," Enriquez continues. "What we worried about was if they would sing."

BELOW: *Taking creative license: lemurs playing on a dinosaur belly. Production still.*

"In the end, we use a lot of science to play fast and loose with science," Schumacher says. "Really informed dinosaur experts—the kids, mostly—will see things that are not accurate. On so many levels, our behind-the-scenes scientific study is vitally important, but we can take all kinds of creative license, because *Dinosaur* is not a documentary. It looks real. It's not real."

Schumacher grins contemplatively. "*Dinosaur* is no more a lesson in paleontology than *The Incredible Mr. Limpet* is a lesson in ichthyology."

THE UNITED STATES IS A VERITABLE FOSSIL JAMBOREE, WITH SIGNIFICANT FINDS IN COLORADO, WYOMING, UTAH, SOUTH DAKOTA, OKLAHOMA, AND MONTANA.

THE SCIENCE OF STORYTELLING

Initial development for *Dinosaur*, however, did resemble an elaborate collegiate paleontology lab. The creative, story, design, and technical teams engaged in extensive study of the latest scientific findings: extinction theories, fossil skeletal structures, hypotheses of dinosaur musculatures and dermatology; and data of prehistoric astronomy, geology, ecology, agriculture, and meteorology. "If this world was going to be real to our audiences," Marsden explains, "first it had to be real to us."

Since the proof-of-concept test, the idea of *Dinosaur* had been to cast CGI characters in a dimensionally photographed world. Schumacher recalls, "We looked at building the sets as miniatures that we could keep on sound stages so we would have both flexibility and control."

Visual effects supervisor Neil Krepela had been working for effects house Boss Film Studios before he came to the *Dinosaur* team. "I still have the blueprint somewhere of a Lockheed building down the street, an old wing assembly plant. We were going to put in fourteen stages and a giant model shop. We planned to shoot on seven stages and build or tear down on seven, and rotate these cameras around on overhead gantries. We would have raised the roof on one section, and we had a pit designed for the other section to get under the sets. It was humongous."

BELOW: *Visual development art by Mark Hallett.*

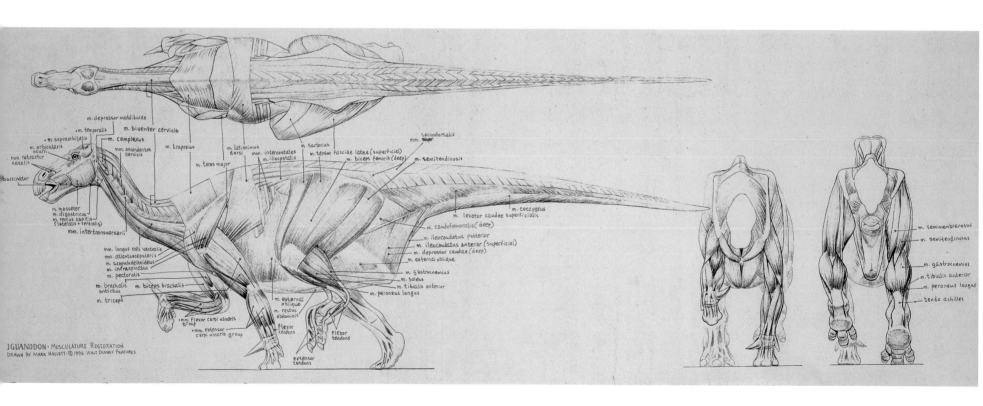

IGUANODON · MUSCULATURE RESTORATION
DRAWN BY MARK HALLETT ©1996 WALT DISNEY FEATURES

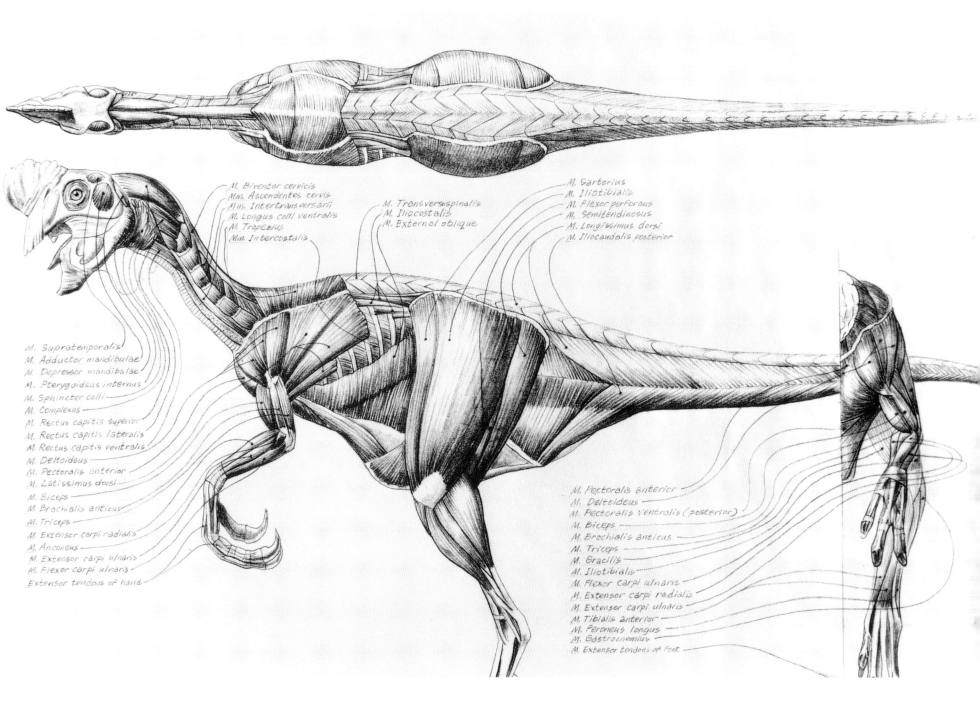

M. Biventer cervicis
Mm. Ascendentes cervis
Mm. Intertransversarii
M. Longus colli ventralis
M. Trapezius
Mm. Intercostalis

M. Transversospinalis
M. Iliocostalis
M. External oblique

M. Sartorius
M. Iliotibialis
M. Flexor perforans
M. Semitendinosus
M. Longissimus dorsi
M. Iliocaudalis posterior

M. Supratemporalis
M. Adductor mandibulae
M. Depressor mandibulae
M. Pterygoideus internus
M. Sphincter colli
M. Complexus
M. Rectus capitis superior
M. Rectus capitis lateralis
M. Rectus capitis ventralis
M. Deltoideus
M. Pectoralis anterior
M. Latissimus dorsi
M. Biceps
M. Brachialis anticus
M. Triceps
M. Extensor carpi radialis
M. Anconeus
M. Extensor carpi ulnaris
M. Flexor carpi ulnaris
Extensor tendons of hand

M. Pectoralis anterior
M. Deltoideus
M. Pectoralis ventralis (posterior)
M. Biceps
M. Brachialis anticus
M. Triceps
M. Gracilis
M. Iliotibialis
M. Flexor carpi ulnaris
M. Extensor carpi radialis
M. Extensor carpi ulnaris
M. Tibialis anterior
M. Peroneus longus
M. Gastrocnemius
M. Extensor tendons of foot

ABOVE: *Visual development art by Mark Hallett.*

Visual FX supervisor Terry Moews (pronounced "MAYS") picks up the story. "Then we would engineer everything in the computer—the ground plane, the background geometry, which would be used to build the model. Then the model would go on the stage. Then the camera moves would all be written in the computer and we would just translate them to the stage, and run the stages day and night, night and day for a year, and then we'd have all the backgrounds for the movie. Right?"

Wrong. Moews admits, "Now, in theory, that's perfect. The problem is that physical reality just does not mimic the ease of design that you find in the CG world. It just doesn't work. Physical properties expand and contract with cold and heat. Blueprints err by one or two inches. Everything changes. Nothing can be done with the exactitude that you work with in the computer. And so what you find is, it's all built—and it doesn't work."

LEFT: *Visual development art by Walter Martishius.*

ABOVE AND BELOW: *Visual development art by Doug Henderson.*

DILIGENT STUDY
GENERATES EXQUISITE ART

By late 1995, the production staff was beginning its move into the new Northside Studio facility. While one group struggled with story, another brainstormed methods for photorealistic backgrounds and settings. Yet another team was deeply involved in adapting existing software and developing new technology to create the world of *Dinosaur*. Marsden, Zondag, Leighton, Bloodworth, and company traveled among the teams, offering input and keeping communication flowing. Production designer Walter Martishius,

LEFT: *Visual development art by David Krentz.*

BELOW: *Visual development art by Ian Gooding.*

art director Cristy Maltese, and literally dozens of artists began working out *Dinosaur* visual concepts in all manner of media.

There is a common misconception that the complex and technical vision of computer animation begins and ends in the digital domain. The opposite is true. Like all animated features, *Dinosaur* began with the traditional tools of drawing and painting: pastels, markers, paint, and pencil.

ABOVE: *Visual development art by Eric McLean.*

LEFT: *Visual development art of a gliding lizard by Christophe Vacher.*

ABOVE RIGHT: *Visual development art of a pteranodon. Drawing by David Krentz; painting by Christophe Vacher.*

ABOVE: *Visual development art of a parasaurolophus by Ricardo Delgado.*

The dinosaur characters and settings were brought to life by cutting-edge computer technology, but all were designed—from the color of hides to the structure of faces, from the angle of light to the color of a sunset—to create believable personalities and locations, while augmenting the moods and goals of the story.

TOP LEFT: *Color art for Kron, Neera and Aladar by Walter Martishius.*

LEFT: *Herd drawing by Mark Hallett; painting by Walter Martishius.*

BELOW: *Colored story sketches by Walter Martishius.*

DINOSAUR
PRODUCTION DESIGN

Walt Disney Feature Animation

4

COLOR OUTLINE

people are accustomed to seeing in a live-action movie. So you can't push things as far as you do in traditional animation, because people just won't buy it—it won't approximate a live-action movie. And, believe me, coming from my animation experience, there are things that I want to do all the time that I just can't do."

DIFFERENCES IN DESIGN

Although Feature Animation took a complete departure with the idea of photorealistic design, "the roots are exactly same," says Maltese. "Our process starts out the same way a traditionally animated film does, then it takes a different production path. But the *look* of it—the feel, the tone of it—is very different from what I'm used to. The people from the live-action side say the same thing."

The key difference for Maltese and her crew to remember was that although they were working on an animated feature, it would *represent* live action. "We actually made a point of pushing our look at the outset," says Maltese, "knowing that it would get collapsed somewhat by the live-action 'look.' The design approach is affected by what

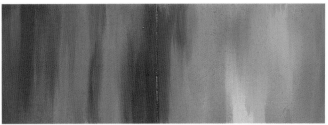

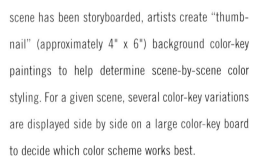

Color Keys

One of the subtlest touches in animated film design—something that audiences rarely notice, but often can feel—is that of a film's color palette. Once a scene has been storyboarded, artists create "thumbnail" (approximately 4" x 6") background color-key paintings to help determine scene-by-scene color styling. For a given scene, several color-key variations are displayed side by side on a large color-key board to decide which color scheme works best.

Throughout this visual development process, Baker Bloodworth remembers seeing concept art going up on the walls at Northside. "You'd go through the halls and people would be buzzing, 'How are we going to do this? How are we going to do that? How are we going to make that come to life?' Nobody had done it before; it was incredibly inspiring."

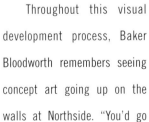

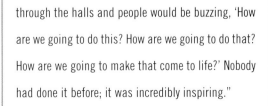

VISUAL DEVELOPMENT

"As art director," Maltese continues, "what I really need to do is make sure that all the visual elements are speaking the same language, and that it carries the story along. Everything you see on screen must support the story, the action, and the dialogue—it should all flow as one. Nothing should be jumping out at you—unless it's *supposed* to be jumping out at you."

"You have to be careful in CGI not to get carried away with 'flying logos,'" Eric Leighton cautions. "For example, saying, 'Boy, isn't this cool, we can move the camera anywhere! We can just zoom it around the planet and then back in through the house and down over here!' That's completely unreal filmmaking—doing things because you *can*. We have a forced reality here to begin with; it needs grounding to meet the audience's perception of filmmaking. As often as possible, we've stuck to a cinematic reality."

TOP: *Visual development art by Cristy Maltese.*

CENTER: *Visual development art by Eric McLean.*

RIGHT: *Visual development art by Robert Mrozowski.*

54

ABOVE: *Visual development art by Robert Mrozowski.*

RIGHT: *Visual development art by Jim Aupperle.*

"There is a certain call to subtlety," Maltese explains. "The less our work is noticed, the more invisible it is, the better. Although designing the look of sequences (What does this look like at night? What does this look like in the daytime?) is quite broad, very fun to do, and often entails a *decreasing* subtlety."

55

ABOVE AND LEFT: *Visual development art by Allen Gonzales.*

BELOW: *Visual development art by Jim Aupperle.*

OPPOSITE TOP: *Color story sketches by Walter Martishius.*

ABOVE AND BELOW: *Multiple design explorations by Allen Gonzales.*

THE FIRST ANIMATED FEATURE FILMED ON LOCATION

By the time, the team had finally arrived at a solution regarding their background and setting problem, they started shooting settings on film in live-action, and dropping the characters into them. "These were not simple still plates," Schumacher says, "but plotted camera moves and angles based on the needs of the story. This offered us the ability to find the most exotic, the most picturesque, the most prehistoric settings anywhere in the world, and use them to create that extra level of photorealism we were seeking."

Walter Martishius, Cristy Maltese, and their crew worked to develop Location Concept Art. "It started with the story sketches," Maltese says. "Then the directors discussed the type of terrain that they wanted, and we'd come up with reference images from books and magazines and create designs based on those—all of that went into the mix. Then our location scout went out to find something that fit with what we had envisioned."

LOCATION DEVELOPMENT: LOCATION SCOUTING

Renowned location scout Dow Griffith was brought to the *Dinosaur* team as supervising location manager. He provided research materials from which the production team could choose locations, then served as a contact with the location property authorities, who worked with him to execute shooting permits, contracts, and other details of the shoot.

Terry Moews, digital artist and visual effects supervisor of the background unit of *Dinosaur*, supervised plate photography, lighting computer-generated characters, and applying and creating live camera moves to shots in the film. On past projects, Moews has filled such roles as plate cameraman, plate camera assistant, motion control programmer, and stage effects supervisor. He also worked back-to-back on films that won Academy Awards for visual effects: *The Abyss* (1989) and *Total Recall* (1990).

HOW'D THEY DO IT?

"The story is broken down on a shot for shot level—it's 'previsualized,'" Moews explains. "We have what we call a 3-D Workbook, which is a 3-D video storyboard. So Pam and the directors know *what* they want to see, and they know how they want to see it, in terms of whether it's a moving shot, or if the camera angle is low or high. My team's job was to take this previsualization, and translate that into a physical environment . . . that we'd never been to.

"We'd go out to location and prescout everything—lay all the shots out beforehand, and we set the shot up with a dummy camera that would just shoot still photos. We also built several video replicas of our film camera systems. We used the same lens, lens mount, everything was the same as our film camera, except it was a video image on a monitor, instead of shooting film. By this means we could stage the action, build it, cut it together, and then see it for ourselves, to see if it worked. We could look at the video, and we'd shoot a lot of pictures, and in that way we could interface with the people back in the Studio."

THE OLDEST KNOWN DINOSAUR FOSSILS HAVE BEEN FOUND IN BRAZIL AND ARGENTINA.

Location shots used in Dinosaur.

TOP: *The Ritual Tree: artificial tree in a real world.*

ABOVE AND LEFT: *On location in Florida (above), Venezuela (left), and California (above left).*

FARAWAY PLACES

Moews and a hard-working motion picture crew known as "First Unit" photographed the mysterious, picturesque, prehistoric locations and settings on film. Another crew, called "Exotic Unit," went to get, well, more exotic shots at more exotic locales: Port Campbell, Australia; Wadi Rum, Jordan; Canaima, Venezuela; and Matareva Beach and Lalopapa Beach in western Samoa. These background plates were then designed, color styled, refined, relighted, and combined via computer technology, in order to create singular locales that seamlessly integrated with the fabricated reality of all the characters.

ON THE ROAD

Once on location, Moews recalls, "We'd have to imagine dinosaurs thirty, forty feet long or seventy feet high out in the real world and make sure that worked. When the film came back and those characters were put into the environment, we'd have to see that there'd be no unnecessary scaling of the environment. Ultimately, what they see in the size and the sheer physical scope of what they want is attainable, and we got it.

"The other side of the coin is the whole production end of it. First, we had to set all those shots up, and choreograph and lay out the continuity of each shot to the creative satisfaction of the directors. Secondly, we had to figure out our live-action shoot—how are we gonna shoot here? If the shot calls for a dolly, how are we gonna set up a dolly on the side of this cliff?"

THIS PAGE, CLOCKWISE FROM TOP RIGHT: *At work on location;* Dinosaur *custom camera tower; dinosaur bones; dinosaur heads and lemur cutouts.*

61

VISION VERSUS REALITY

"We did not bring a trailer full of lights and a team of electricians and gaffers and stuff out there to do this," Moews continues. "We had the sunlight and that's all. A lot of times we'd find ourselves trying to match a very specific preconceived desire and find that, well—the sun was coming from the wrong side."

Moews and his crew were intent on providing as much foundational photography as they could for the filmmakers. Moews says, "A lot of times, I would find myself out on weekends, going back to locations just to pick up different angles or larger vistas that might be useful. Sometimes a plate required several takes, so you have all the elements that you need to make the final thing when it comes back and gets digitized."

NO BONUSES

"The disadvantage to this method of filmmaking is that you lose the usual bonuses of a strictly live-action or a strictly animated film," Schumacher says. "In a live-action movie you can take an actor out to the desert and shoot him front, back, sideways, from a crane, from a helicopter—over and over again. If you don't like something, you're in the moment and you can be extemporaneous, and you get a lot of coverage that you can shape. In *Dinosaur*, the live action is the predetermined scenery. Later in the process when we add our animated characters, we'd find out that we wanted five more shots, but were locked in to what we did."

RIGHT: *The combination of live action and animation produced a spectacular stage for the actors of* Dinosaur. *The computer-animated dinosaur Herd acted in live-action settings filmed all over the world.*

Thom Enriquez continues, "Usually in animation, if we have a change of heart right in the middle of production—if we find a character's a lot more funny, or more interesting—we can go back and reanimate. We'll just paint a new background or create a new background angle. But in *Dinosaur*, we had to work within the limitations of reusing the same live-action backgrounds, which made it frustrating when it came to making story alterations. As a result, we'd first try solutions that had more to do with dialogue than action, in order to keep the action—and therefore, the background—the same."

PUTTING IT TOGETHER

Neil Krepela, visual effects supervisor, had the challenge of a dual goal. First, he had to marry the animation and film worlds. Krepela worked to fold together methods used in visual effects, live action, location shooting, and miniature photography. "I'd pick up what I could from Feature Animation, too, and fold that back into the CGI and live-action purview," Krepela says.

"The other big charge I had was just on the 'look' of the picture," Krepela explains, "to work closely with the art director and production designer and make sure it looked as realistic as possible, and that the characters were lit well."

"CHEATERS NEVER PROSPER..."

"In animation, they can just *cheat* all over the place, and the audience forgives it because, well, that's the way an animated film works," Krepela continues. "With *Dinosaur*, the characters are animated—obviously—but it seems like a live-action film. A lot of my job was to make sure that everything fit as realistically as possible. But we had a great fix—even though we had to stay 'real,' we had access to all the methods of animation and CGI. We had incredible control over the lights, for instance. You don't like the way something's lit? They'll just put another light source there. You can't do that in the real world too easily and have it look so real."

Krepela also worked to make the background film as useful and flexible as possible. After scanning the photographic elements into their digital software systems, the filmmakers could manipulate the images with extreme efficiency and imaginative possibilities. Krepela explains, "We'll take two different locations that might be 150 miles apart and put them together in a shot over an entire two sequences. We had two sequences in this little valley, and we shot half in Titus Canyon, miles from the other half by Mount Whitney. We have a background at Disney Ranch and one at the Arboretum that we put together. We also used a lot of matte paintings and 'digital backgrounds' to complete sets. In some shots, we used miniatures. We'd have skies from Florida and shots from Trona. We'd have skies shot on a soundstage in a gunpowder explosion put in Trona shots as well. We'd just mix everything up."

SETTING THE SCENE

Finally, all of the diverse elements that went into creating the digital animation performance venue for the story of *Dinosaur* were ready to come together. The photographic plates were scanned, and the background's dimensions and engineering were married to a digital equivalent within a virtual set. This created the "stage" for the digital characters.

Sounds incredibly complicated, doesn't it? Well, it is. "That was probably the most restrictive thing," Enriquez reflects. "Just the fact that some of the process was so complex that it felt like anything you did might be cost, or time, or manpower prohibitive. But that's also what was so different about it—it became a very satisfying challenge to overcome those things."

"So there you have it," Schumacher thoughtfully summarizes. "Only a madman would have wanted to make a movie this complicated."

Visual Effects Editorial

The Visual Effects Editorial department is responsible for receiving, cataloging, and filing all the film shot by the First and Exotic units. The VFX Editorial process takes the motion picture film and transfers it to the digital domain, determining the length of element footage to be scanned, their sync position relative to each other, and the need for reposition, blow-ups, or other optical effects.

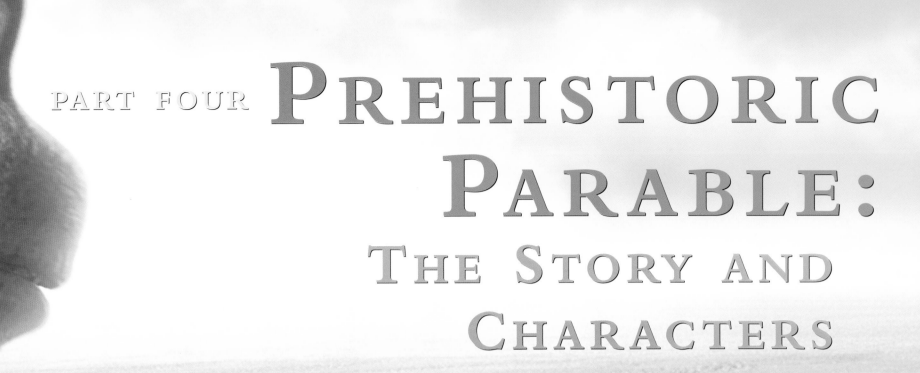

PART FOUR

PREHISTORIC
PARABLE:
THE STORY AND
CHARACTERS

T E L L U S a S T O R Y

ith the *Dinosaur* team in place and the Digital Studio machine up and running, the goal of a photorealistic visual style felt well within reach.

"The movie found itself, like all our movies do," Thom Enriquez says. "It's a very organic process. We start with a concept and we simply find it as we work our way through it. There are so many people involved, that an evolutionary process takes place, and the movie takes on a life of its own."

"Behold the turtle. He makes progress only when he sticks his neck out." —James Bryant Conant

C H A R A C T E R D E S I G N : A D A P T I N G R E A L I T Y

Character designs in computer-generated animation originate much in the same way as traditional animated features: with hand-drawn sketches, paintings, and drawings by a variety of artists. Trying to define the "look" of the characters, the concept artists worked closely with directors Zondag and Leighton.

"When I first heard about the main character of the movie, all I thought was 'As long as it's not an iguanodon, we're okay,'" visual development and character design artist David Krentz chuckles. "The iguanodon is the most plain-jane cow of a dinosaur there is. It's got this big rectangular head and a big rectangular body, and it's just flat-out boring."

Krentz was put in a difficult position on *Dinosaur.* He had pushed, pleaded, cajoled, and threatened his way onto the *Dinosaur* team, due to his lifelong obsession with dinosaurs and their physiognomy. Now he was being asked to alter what fossil evidence had revealed to science about the actual creatures.

TOP LEFT: *Oviraptor by Walter Martishius.*

ABOVE: *Character development art of Aladar by David Krentz.*

OPPOSITE: *Aladar: A hero's face with strong chin, cheekbones and large eyes. Production still.*

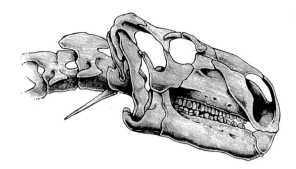

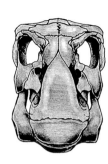

GET OVER IT

"I just had to get over the idea that these are dinosaurs. They aren't," Krentz says. "They're characters. There's walking the line, and there's going over the line. We had to walk the line. They had to be believable as animals, but also believable and interesting as characters. In order to make them read as characters, we really had to push things. And that meant making them very inaccurate dinosaurs."

As the production's resident "dino-geek," Krentz had to find a balance of truth and fantasy that would not only serve the animators but ease his paleontologist's conscience. "The one thing we know about these creatures is their bone structure, and that is constantly debated. For instance, an iguanodon has a little bone over its eye socket. A lot of dinosaurs do, but the iguanadon's is very specific. It's made up of a couple of small pieces that resemble the perfect eyebrow. I read all the journals, papers, and debates I could get my hands on about what this bone did. Then I read a piece where someone said it was probably movable. Bingo! Eyebrows— eye expression . . . I can live with myself now!"

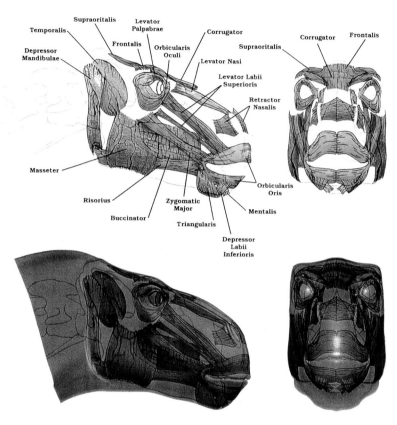

"Then we added the facial muscles of a horse to get facial expression," Krentz explains. "We gave it masseter muscles and all these things for a horsy look. It became really fun to take what's there on the bones, and exaggerate it. That's what animation is all about. We're doing an animated movie here, not a nature film. We used anatomy that could enhance a character."

ABOVE: *The iguanodons's facial expressions were developed by adding movable bony eyebrows and by studying facial muscles of a horse. Development art by Mark Austin and Mark Swain.*

LEFT, TOP AND BOTTOM: *Character development art of Aladar's eye structure by David Krentz.*

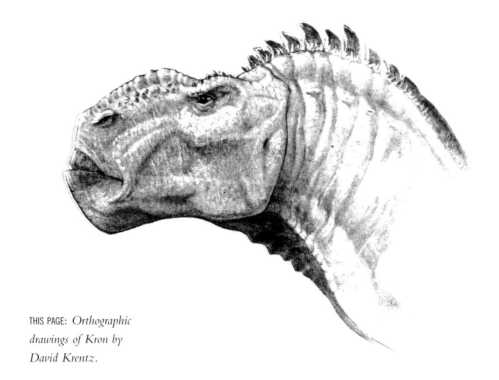

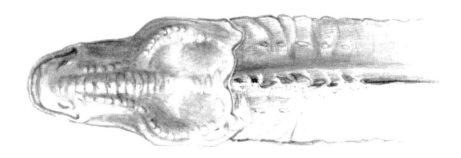

THIS PAGE: *Orthographic drawings of Kron by David Krentz.*

SAME SPECIES, DIFFERENT DINOS

"The other thing was that all the main characters were the same species," Zondag adds. "As soon as you see them in silhouette you wouldn't be able to differentiate characters. No matter how different they are, they all still have this big rectangular head. So we had to distinguish them, and yet keep them in the same family, make them look like the same species. We really had to push their designs. That was a hard one, because you could go too far. We had Bruton with great big rhinoceros plates all over him at one point. It looked really cool, but when you put him up against Neera or Aladar, you'd think, 'Is that the same species?' So we just tried to stay believable.

"We'd add a little bit of bump on the nose, or change the shape of the beak a little. We'd find what we could and exaggerate it. Bruton has that loaf of bread on his nose. And Kron has a powerful neck with a mountain peak in his chin. Aladar has a little bit of a hero face. We gave him more of a chin and some cheekbone, and larger eyes. So as soon as their shapes evolved they started to differentiate from one another."

"Besides," Krentz smiles, "there's plenty of opportunities for accuracy with the Herd animals. Several Herd members are bang-on scientifically accurate. That kept my conscience clear."

NO ONE REALLY KNOWS WHAT COLOR DINOSAURS WERE. THEY MAY HAVE BEEN THE MUTED COLORS OF CROCODILES OR COMMON LIZARDS, OR THEY MAY HAVE BEEN STRIPED LIKE ZEBRAS OR TIGERS.

VOICING CONCERNS

Characters aren't complete without voices. Voices must be carefully chosen to match the behavior, age, and even the shape of a character.

Casting director Ruth Lambert says, "My prerequisite is someone who either brings a great persona into the room, or someone with a great, interesting voice. A lot of times my directors can get distracted, oddly enough, by an actor's physicality. Sometimes you do get distracted if they're . . . fabulous-looking. I mean, wouldn't you?" Lambert laughs. "We listen later and make sure that we're not being distracted by how fabulous-looking someone is. In order to avoid these physical distractions and concentrate on voice performance, everyone in the room has their head down, or turns around or puts something in front of their faces—which is a little disconcerting for a poor actor who's used to having people pay attention. So I make sure that the actor has one person in the room who's looking right at them, and that's usually me."

Voices are chosen carefully to express each character in the film:

OPPOSITE: Yar, the curmudgeonly patriarch of the lemur clan, and the youthful Suri. Production still.

RIGHT: The formidable Herd leader Kron and his right-hand man, Bruton. Production still.

BELOW: The misfits of the Herd. Production still.

TAKE TWELVE

Voice performances are recorded before the animation is done, because the delivery and timing of the lines will influence the "acting" that the animator brings to the character. Often, a voice actor will bring a further development to the character that hadn't been planned. A gesture, a different attitude, even the individual personality of the voice actor will influence the way the animator creates the performance of the character.

"Over the production period of an animated film, a voice actor records and re-records all the time, sometimes half a dozen times, sometimes more," Lambert explains.

DIGITAL DOLLS

Every character in the film is created as a three-dimensional object, or model, within the computer, like a digital sculpture or doll. The digital sculptors are responsible for creating these models for all of the 3-D characters in the film. They begin with 2-D orthographic drawings (and sometimes use 3-D sculptures for reference). Then the final designs are executed inside the computer. The key difference between the digital sculptor and the traditional sculptor is tools—the digital sculptor uses mathematical equations instead of clay.

During this process, the modeling department works closely with the directors, animators, and character designers to ensure that the character's design is as streamlined and efficient as possible.

Unlike traditional cel animation, in which the animator finalizes the character design and "makes it move" through individual drawings, the computer animation process is split into two steps: the building of the character and the animating of the character. The modeler creates the finished character model within the computer and then passes it on to the animator, who brings the character to life.

The animators make the characters move by controls on the model. This is still a painstaking frame-by-frame process, but instead of drawing each action of the character, the animator uses the computer controls like marionette strings to control each movement of the character, from a cross-frame walk to the lift of an eyebrow.

A DINOSAUR of FEW WORDS, Ankylo is HEAVILY fortified in his armour, so he's fearless/oblivious of any THREAT

ARMOUR CLATTERS like KNIGHT OR SAMURAI WHEN it WALKS.

ANKYLOSAUR
THE DINOSAUR PROJECT
RICARDO DELGADO
12.96

TOP: *Orthographic drawings of Url by David Krentz.*

LEFT: *Character development art of an ankylosaur by Ricardo Delgado.*

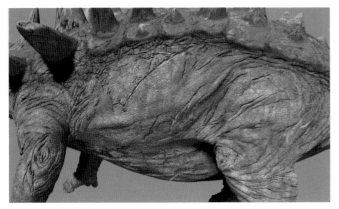

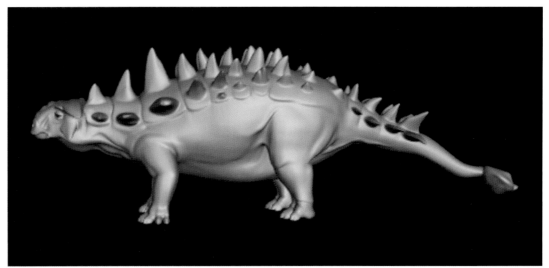

TOP RIGHT: *Final approved drawings of a character are given to the computer modelers who create a basic, smooth model. The animators then use this model to bring a character to life.*
ABOVE: *Muscles, skin, textures, and color are added to the model.*

LEFT, TOP TO BOTTOM: *Special challenges in the computer animation of Url: wrinkles around the eyes have to move when Url blinks and uses his mouth; the mouth has to include gums, teeth, and tongue; shaders are added to the model to give the illusion of "wetness" around Url's nostrils and eyes; the skin on the underbelly has to meet and merge with the hard shell; and the wrinkles around the legs have to move with the sagging, stretching skin caused by walking.*

ANI-MOTION

The *Dinosaur* animators came from traditional hand-drawn, clay animation, and stop-motion animation backgrounds, as well as CGI experience, and a mix of all of those methods. Supervising animator Mark Anthony Austin explains, "The major difference between traditional and CG animation is that traditional animation focuses on the study of acting. Traditional animators take that study of acting and embellish it to make it fuller, richer, more exaggerated. But CG animation focuses more on motion as opposed to acting. For example, focusing on how far something can move, regardless of acting. The key with *Dinosaur* was to merge these two schools of thought."

IT'S NOT REALISM IN MOTION, IT'S REALISM IN STANDING STILL

Austin further explains, "The understanding in traditional animation is ultimately 'fluidity of movement,' where errors are somewhat obvious to all viewers, regardless of their experience or background, and the 'flatness' of color helps to disguise any lack of movement. Hence, 'holds' (where the character remains motionless for any amount of time) go virtually unnoticed.

"In computer animation a fluid motion can be achieved without effort—such is the mathematical capability of the technology. This 'free motion' can lead to laziness on the part of an animator working in 'special effects,' in which case breaking the fluidity requires much more effort.

"It is important for an animator to realize that the added texture (in the character's skin, for example) provides more visual information, so any glitches in motion or lack of motion become immediately apparent. It is the 'detailing,' or the layering of motion, the adding of surface movement (which is then displayed by the texture) that can be detrimental to the illusion. It is this 'finishing' that either sells the animation or breaks the fantasy."

"It is nice to be able to return to a scene and polish up rough edges," supervising animator Trey Thomas agrees. "In stop-motion, you get one shot at it—if you have one bad frame, you have to live with it. That's pretty brutal. It's nice to be able to use the computer to finesse stuff and soften it out. But I think a lot of people go too far in that direction—smoothing and polishing everything so much that it looks inorganic. The resulting images don't have the flaws of real life."

With the beginnings of character animation, all the elements of *Dinosaur* were finally in place to tell the story.

THIS PAGE: *Working from existing, low-resolution computer models of their characters, the Dinosaur animators created key frames of animation (above). Once the animation is approved, the muscle, skin, and textures are then applied to the key frame models to create the final frames (right).*

he Story

Dinosaur opens in a panoramic spectacle. After a fearsome and violent carnotaur attack, a lone, orphaned iguanodon egg is kidnapped from its nest by a hungry oviraptor. During a fight with another dinosaur over the egg, the oviraptor accidentally drops it into a river. The egg is swept through the water until it plunges over a waterfall. A giant pteranodon snatches the egg from the boiling water and carries it off, only to be startled by a flock of icthyornis. The pteranodon loses its grip on the egg, which finally falls into a tree on an island without dinosaurs, where a community of lemurs lives.

The lemur clan's reaction toward the mysterious egg changes from fear and uncertainty to protection and support when a vulnerable baby dinosaur hatches out of the shell. The newborn iguanodon is adopted by the clan's matriarch, Plio, despite the reservations of her father, Yar. They name him Aladar, and raise him as one of their own.

ABOVE: *A giant pteranadon soars off with the iguanadon egg that will become Aladar. Production still.*

Beautiful Plio—gentle, kind, and maternal.

TOP RIGHT: *Character development art by David Krentz.*

BELOW: *Character development art of Plio by Ricardo Delgado.*

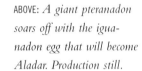

PLIO: ROCK-STEADY EARTH MOTHER

Plio is the matriarch of the lemur clan, a kindhearted peacemaker whose gentle wisdom embodies the compassion of the lemurs. Her counsel guides the lemur community in their daily activity and saves the infant iguanodon, Aladar. Through Plio's actions, Aladar learns the value of family and working together, welcoming even the strangest of creatures into his heart.

Trey Thomas, Plio's supervising animator, says, "Lemurs were the pre-simians right before primates. No other creatures like them lived during the dinosaur period. When I came here I was so excited about the whole thing, I went hog-wild and took a vacation to Madagascar and studied and photographed lemurs."

Thomas's research became something of an animation double-edged sword. "Animating lemurs was a unique challenge because no one was familiar with their particular movement," Thomas explains. "Roy Disney said of the lemurs, 'they hop around funny,' and they do. No one is really familiar with that style of locomotion—so I'm not sure if audiences will identify with it or if it will just look strange. It's kind of a tightrope we're walking. Their movement is bizarre-looking, even though it's absolutely realistic."

"Of the lemurs, Plio is the most realistic and the most subdued," Thomas says of his character. "I work more with subtleties—that's more my personality. The other animators who supervised lemurs came from a traditional background, so they were more inclined toward cartoony timings and poses. But that was appropriate for those characters, because Zini and Yar and Suri are more caricatured, and Plio had to remain the link to the 'real' lemur world. She's the one who grounds all the rest of them, so she had to be the most realistic and subdued."

Thomas felt that Alfre Woodard hit the mark performing Plio's voice. "Alfre was certainly emotionally real, and subdued, just the way Plio is written and intended. She has a nice, warm, motherly quality to her voice."

Woodard had no difficulty identifying with Plio as a mother. "I am very happy to be a part of something that I know my children will be impressed by. I really watch what they watch, and am very mindful of what they're hearing and seeing all the time, and my children are very bright, and engaging, and interesting, and I think I have been involved in something that my children deserve to see."

BELOW: *Plio peers guardedly at the new arrival to Lemur Island. Production still.*

YAR: "CURMUDGEONLINESS"

Yar is Plio's father, the feisty elder statesman of the lemur clan. Although officially retired, he can't help sticking his nose into everybody's business. His gruff, curmudgeonly exterior is a thin veil for his warm heart. Despite his gruff stubbornness—and although he would never admit to it—Yar is probably the most sentimental and emotional of the lemur clan.

Lambert recalls casting Yar's voice. "They wanted the voice actor to carry a certain gruffness, but have the ability to communicate that 'heart of gold' quality. He wasn't menacing, as much as warm, and even funny. Yar's gruffness and his curmudgeonliness, if that's even a word, well, Ossie Davis was able to create that."

Davis understood Yar immediately. "Though he is big-of-mouth when he senses what he thinks is an intrusion on his authority, he is also

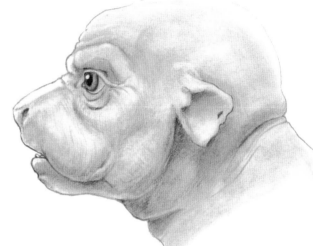

Wild-maned Yar: grizzled and grumbling on the outside, a softy on the inside.

ABOVE AND RIGHT: *Orthographic drawing of Yar by David Krentz.*

BELOW: *Character development art by David Krentz.*

warm-hearted and sympathetic," the actor explains. "He's a grandfatherly figure, and from my own experience—I, too am a grandfather—that part of him gives me no difficulty whatsoever!"

BAD HAIR DAYS

One of the most impressive attributes of the lemur characters was the software program created to represent their fur. As good as it finally looked, it initially presented a problem to the animators. "We animate the lemurs in a very crude geometrical form," Trey Thomas explains, "because the data weight of the scenes have to be workable. So in

ABOVE AND RIGHT:
Production stills.

ABOVE: *Plio, Yar, and Suri character development art by Tina Price.*

animation, the lemurs don't have fur. They don't have absolute values—only a silhouette. So as we're animating it looks really nice, but sometimes when these things get furred and finalized, it doesn't look like what we originally had animated. It was hard to get a handle on what it would finally look like. At first, that was a real pain in the butt. After a while, though, as we got a feel for it, we could anticipate what it was going to look like and make adjustments."

he Story Continues...

Years pass, and Aladar grows up with
the love and inspiration of his adoptive
family. Aladar's friends are all young
lemurs, including Plio's daughter, Suri,
and the energetic young Zini. One day,
Plio hurries the youngsters along to the
lemur festivities, the annual courtship
ceremony. Aladar, Plio, Yar, and Suri
watch the courtship ritual, where young
lemur couples pair up. At the end,
only Zini is left without a mate and
is consoled by Aladar. Plio realizes that
Aladar, too, has no mate.

ABOVE: *Aladar watches the*
annual lemur courting
ritual. Production still.

ZINI: I WAS A TEEN-AGE LEMUR LOTHARIO

Zini is a young adult lemur with an accent on the "young." He's a bundle of energy who's always eager to lend a hand in a tough situation, but whose natural clumsiness occasionally gets him into trouble. Zini fancies himself something of a smooth operator—unfortunately, he's not as much a hit with the ladies as he imagines, but this reality never sinks in. It is Zini who winds up as the young iguanadon's best pal. "He's me with fur and hairdo," supervising animator Bill Fletcher grins.

"Of all the characters on the show, he's had the most turmoil," Fletcher says. "I really don't think they knew what to do with him. They knew we needed a comic character. At first he was supposed

The young and excitable Zini:
the not-so-smooth lady's man.

ABOVE: *Production stills.*

BELOW: *Visual development art*
by Ralph Zondag.

ZINI

ABOVE: *Character development art by Eric Goldberg.*

RIGHT: *Character development art by David Krentz.*

to be mute, and I thought that was pretty challenging, comedy through body language.

"But I love to do the lip sync," Fletcher says. "You've got something to jump off of when you have a good voice. So then we decided, mute's not going to work, let's have Zini talk. So we went through a whole bunch of different voices, and none of them really clicked."

"Zini didn't speak at all for a long time," Lambert says. "Then when he started to speak, his character wasn't landing."

"Until one day they sought out Max Casella," Fletcher says.

"Max was in *The Lion King* on Broadway," Lambert explains. "Tom Schumacher said, 'Just hire Max.' We were lucky: Max wanted to do it."

Casella helped Zini's character evolve for the story team and for Fletcher. "I could never get into the other voices that were suggested. But Max really clicked, and Zini evolved into a better character because of it. Zini's a guy who isn't aware of what a misfit he is or how goofy he is. He thinks the girls love him, that he's Mr. Smooth."

"He's a love-monkey," Max Casella laughs. "He loves life, lives life to the fullest . . . even though life keeps throwing obstacles in his way all the time."

Casella has truly brought his own upbeat spirit to his performance as Zini, and has treasured the experience. "This is the best job," the young actor admits. "Disney is the king of animation, so they really know what they're doing, and I love coming in here."

SURI WITH THE FRINGE ON TOP

Suri is the prepubescent pistol of the lemurs—furry, feisty, inquisitive, candid, and typically eight years old. She especially loves to play with her 3-ton big brother, Aladar. When the lemurs's world changes, Suri clings to her one source of security—her mother, Plio.

Supervising animator Larry White says, "I was intrigued with the character because she was playful. She's cute and innocent, but at the same time a little mischievous. I found a lot of entertainment value in that, and I tried to find ways of interjecting some of that playfulness throughout the film. The main thing I wanted to do was keep her very child-like. There was a tendency on this film, obviously, toward realism, but because of my traditional animation background I tried to make sure that Suri retained more of the kind of anthropomorphic characteristics that I'm used to seeing in 2-D."

Hayden Panettiere had impressed Lambert with her work as Princess Dot in *A Bug's Life*. "She's very natural and I just love her. When this 'little girl,' Suri, happened, we tried a couple of other little girls. Then I said, 'Let's just try Hayden,' so that's what we did, and she's adorable."

RIGHT: *Character development art by Ralph Zondag.*

A TAIL OF TWO MEDIA

White even found a way to apply his hand-drawn animation skills to CGI. "Since I'm quick at gesturing out animation on paper, I started a system where I could use our pencil test machine, rough out a scene on paper, digitize it, transfer it into the computer, bring it up as a Rotoscope image, and use that as a pattern for movement."

White found this system particularly useful with the lemur tails. "If I had a very complicated scene, or a very complicated tail pattern, I would animate the tail on paper and get all the complicated moves down and match the moves up based on the patterns that I had drawn. That must have saved weeks' worth of work on a complicated move."

BELOW: *Character development art by Thom Enriquez.*

"She was very fun," White says of Panettiere. "She's an exuberant little girl, and I really love her voice. I thought I could draw a lot of emotion out of it. And the playfulness—I love her laugh. It actually inspired me to do some visual things with the character. There's one part near the courtship sequence where Suri is just excited and happy, she runs in and turns and laughs and giggles and turns and jumps out again. It's one of my favorite scenes because it's a good representation of what I was trying to pull off with the character. The voice was such a good starting point for me. I was able to carry that bubbly attitude in the visuals."

ALADAR: CONFIDENT, CHARISMATIC OUTSIDER

Aladar, the iguanodon, is the confident, charismatic, playful hero of *Dinosaur*—the mischievous camp counselor every kid wishes he had. Orphaned in a carnotaur attack and raised by gentle lemurs, Aladar is awed by his first encounter with the Herd of dinosaurs, but soon finds that their brutal and intractable "survival of the fittest" outlook is at odds both with the compassionate nature of the lemurs who raised him—and the resilient adaptability that will be imperative to their survival.

Aladar's appeal springs from his outsiders' point of view—both his ability to see things objectively, and his concurrent frustration in trying to change the inflexible views and actions of his community.

Thomas Schumacher explains, "There's a terrific strength that comes from this idea of a society joining together, comprehending its adversity and trying to conquer it, trying to rise above it and live through it. There's also a suspense there—will Aladar be able to effect some kind of change?"

Supervising animator Mark Anthony Austin faced a peculiar predicament. "Even though he's the lead character, my challenge was to make him interesting. I know that sounds odd, but Aladar is in a neutral area the hero often occupies. He can't be too diverse. He can't be too angry. He can't be too zany. That can be very limiting as an animator—you have to make them as interesting as you can, because they're on screen the most. That's probably the biggest challenge with any of the 'hero' or 'lead' characters—to try and keep them from being dull, because they can't be too extreme in either direction. It's a fine balance."

D. B. Sweeney provided the earnest voice of Aladar. "We didn't audition all that many people," Lambert recalls. "We just wanted to find someone who sounded decent, young, and enthusiastic, whose performance could help Mark carry the character over those bland spots. The funny thing is, Sweeney and Ralph Zondag sound a lot alike, and Ralph always leaned toward guys who sort of sounded like him. I don't even think he knew that he was doing it, but it happened again and again and again. So Sweeney does sound a little bit like Ralph. There's an earnestness to him that Ralph has."

"I wouldn't have thought of Sweeney," Austin says. "But I'm biased now, having worked with him, because he's such a genuinely nice guy.

Aladar: the gentle hero.

OPPOSITE LEFT: *Production still.*

OPPOSITE CENTER: *Baby Aladar character development art by David Krentz.*

TOP, LEFT AND RIGHT: *Character development art by David Krentz.*

BELOW: *Character development art by Ralph Zondag.*

ABOVE: *Aladar flees.*
Production still.

ABOVE AND LEFT:
Production stills.

icking Up the Story...

Overall, life seems quite content for is odd little family on Lemur Island, ntil catastrophe strikes—a huge meteor llides with the earth.

The explosion destroys Lemur land, forcing the only survivors, Aladar nd his immediate family of lemurs, to a nd across the sea. Their future appears bleak as this new land. Strange crea- res they've never seen before stalk em. Danger is imminent.

Lost and tired, they escape from peril y uniting with a large herd of dinosaurs ey encounter trudging wearily across e devastated landscape.

Aladar is astounded to encounter his vn kind. However, conflict arises etween Aladar and Kron, the Herd's ader, as everything Aladar does to help e Herd either infuriates Kron or allenges his authority.

"The other huge challenge with Aladar," Austin continues, "was the fact that he is a dinosaur and he has to be realistic. Because of the proportions of his face, it was hard to make him act in a very characteristic manner. The whole basis of character animation is the relationship between the eyes and the mouth, how a human face works. But Aladar, from the orthographic view, originally had his eyes on the side so you couldn't actually get that relationship. So we had to cheat the bone structure. We worked with paleontologists on what we could get away with on the bone structure. We didn't want to divert too far from what they could have looked like . . . even though we did make some drastic changes."

KRON: A LEADER IN CRISIS

ABOVE: *Kron character development art by David Krentz.*

Kron is the fierce iguanodon chief of the dinosaur Herd, a leader at home with "the way things have always been done." Now that ecological disaster has forever changed the Herd's route to their traditional Nesting Grounds, Kron finds himself incapable of adapting to a changed world. He conceals his trepidation and doubt behind a façade of self-assured authority. It's a thin masquerade that can't withstand the ever-increasing challenges of the journey . . . and the arrival of a more compassionate and innovative leader named Aladar.

"What interested me about Kron was that I didn't see him as a villain at all," supervising animator Eamonn Butler asserts. "I kind of saw him as a fallen hero. I found anchors for the character that I could envision. Here's a guy who's lived in fear most of his life: always on the run, living in fear of terrifying creatures, being forced out of his home, always moving. What would you turn into? Kron has had to become tough to survive.

"He's also the biggest, strongest, best-looking guy in the Herd—the alpha male—but it's a constant struggle for leadership, because he's always being challenged for that position. So not only does he face threat from the external predators, he's facing a constant challenge to his position from within the Herd.

"So here's a guy who lives in a very hostile environment. Everywhere he goes there's a challenge and a threat. So I gave him this determination. If he has to get the Herd somewhere he's gotta get them there no matter what—even if that means sacrificing some of the weak. I thought that made him strong but fallible. To me that was heroic in its own way.

"I want to show that power and that strength, but the medium doesn't allow us to use the tricks that we use when we animate in other styles, and a lot of the shots were framed to show just head and neck. So, whatever you've got on screen, you use it.

*Kron: the merciless
leader of the Herd.*

"I listened to the dialogue and it's very direct. I thought, 'How am I gonna make him threatening even when you only see his face?'

"Kron wears leadership like a suit, and a suit tells you something about the guy who wears it. I thought, 'Maybe Kron could feel uncomfortable within his own skin, uncomfortable wearing the mantle of leadership. Maybe he could also use that, use his mass, what he wears, to threaten people.' So in the animation we could move his head around quite fast, giving some snap to his movement, and then letting the neck follow through, so when he stops moving, his neck carries on. That tells the audience, 'He's huge. That's alotta meat back there on his neck.' And by showing that he's comfortable with this, he's subtly telling you, 'I'm bigger and stronger than you.' That really helped to sell an understated power in Kron—a simple animation technique. We also played with the facial animation in a big way. If you look at Kron he's very well-defined. There's a lot of musculature under there."

90

Bruton: a loyal lieutenant.

ABOVE: *Production still.*

BOTTOM RIGHT: *Character development art by Thom Enriquez.*

Another part of Kron's subtle power came from the voice performance of Samuel E. Wright. Ruth Lambert recalls, "We had another actor originally cast, but the character of Kron changed dramatically, and suddenly the voice didn't make any sense. Sam Wright was in *The Lion King* on Broadway, and we hired him and it worked out great. He's got that beautiful voice."

It's a far cry from the character voice that made him famous, but Wright brings strength and authority to the role of Kron with the same dexterity and expertise that made his voice of Caribbean crab Sebastian in *The Little Mermaid* (1989) one for the ages. Wright's remarkable versatility also earned him a Tony nomination for his performance as Mufasa in the Broadway musical *The Lion King*.

A lifelong Disney fan, Wright is actually humbled by his contribution to the Disney legacy. "I've worked for Disney for years," the actor explains, "and I love working with them because they're dedicated to the detail it requires to make a masterpiece—a lasting work."

"He's an incredibly versatile actor," says Butler, "and probably one of the most professional people I've ever met. Every single take, without fail, he would bring something new to a line of dialogue."

BRUTON: OLD SOLDIERS NEVER DIE

Proud, no-nonsense Bruton is Kron's right-hand man, a battle-hardened career "lieutenant" who dutifully follows the traditional ways of the Herd. Initially distrustful of Aladar's rag-tag group of lemurs and Herd Misfits, Bruton is affected by their kindness and generosity.

"He's a heavy," supervising animator Dick Zondag admits of Bruton, "but you kind of feel bad for this guy. He could be any of us. You can't blame him for the way he is—it's the way he is. This is life. He's supposed to uphold law and order. He's like an old soldier, or an old policeman, and only at the bitter end does he realize that maybe he was wrong—or his way was wrong.

"It was fun being able to go there and work with the part of his persona that comes from just being older, and using that battle-worn, weary

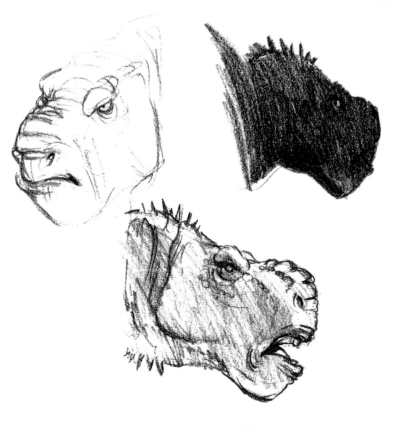

eyes were so small. You look at his face and you're mesmerized by the details. Is this going to hurt his performance? So I made some conscious decisions. I would animate his eyes first, and leave everything else alone, so that you understood him through his eyes."

Zondag's macro solution was related to Butler's physical performance of Kron, only Zondag took it in another direction. "We designed Bruton as big and overweight. Where Eamonn used Kron's size and mass to portray his power, we actually downplayed Bruton's muscle inertia and played up the synergy, so that what we got was a loose, flabby feeling. When he moves, he has a hard time controlling his own weight. The result is almost a stagger—you can see, you can feel he's tired. We brought that palpable fatigue to both his body movement and to his character."

The addition of Peter Siragusa as Bruton's voice added to the effect. Zondag explains, "Peter's voice is gruff, and it's got this very 'blue collar' sound to it, which is exactly what Bruton is. He's this very plainspoken working stiff. At the same time, you get a sense of humanity, you understand he's probably not that bad of a guy. There's an underlying hope with him. With Kron, there is no hope—he is what he is, and he's not going to change."

More Story ...

Zini points out Neera to Aladar, suggesting that she would make a good mate, and embarrasses Aladar in front of Neera. Kron tells Bruton to warn the Herd not to lag behind, as no one will help rescue them.

TOP: *Production still.*

CENTER: *Orthographic drawings of Bruton by David Krentz.*

aspect of his character. It's taking that hard military stereotype and raking it over to find there's something else in there. But Bruton doesn't turn around completely. He's still got a hard edge, even at the very end. However, his philosophy has been changed."

Zondag found similar challenges to those Butler and Austin describe, in coaxing a believable performance from such an imposing character. His solution was twofold: "micro" and "macro." Zondag admits, "I was very nervous that Bruton's

LEFT: *Character development art of Neera by Ian Gooding.*

LEFT AND BELOW: *Bruton. Production Stills.*

NO-NONSENSE NEERA

Neera is Kron's scrupulous sister. She's as capable as her brother is, but she has a greater capacity for courage and compassion. The traditional values she shares with her brother are challenged when she meets Aladar, whose strange ways intrigue Neera and trigger a transformation that culminates in a heart-wrenching decision to defy her brother and follow Aladar.

Supervising animator Joel Fletcher had to deal with a dual shift in the character of Neera. "Originally Neera was a lot more of a spoiled princess–type character, and as the story developed, she became a much stronger, deeper character."

Fletcher continues, "Because of the photo-realism of this movie, the animation became a lot more like real acting, definitely subtle. Neera has very fine facial features, so I often had to restrain myself. I'd always overdo it on the first pass, then I'd have to reel it in a bit to get her expressions and acting right—and that's just for the facial stuff.

The Story Continues...

In the back of the Herd are the slowest dinosaurs, the outcasts—the misfits. Aladar learns that the Herd is going to its annual Nesting Grounds, a place much like the Lemur Island.

The Herd travels across the desert to a familiar watering spot, only to discover that it has dried up. Aladar finds water while trying to help the ailing Eema. Kron bullies his way to the water, and the Herd follows his lead. Neera watches from afar as Aladar helps Eema away from the chaos and pandemonium—while her brother and the others greedily drink. This newcomer Aladar has piqued her interest. A romantic interest builds between the two of them.

Just as they're getting to know each other, Bruton tells Kron about nearby carnotaurs. Kron decides to move the Herd out. Aladar expresses concern for the ones at the back who can't keep up. Kron coldly replies that that is their purpose, to slow down the predators. When Aladar challenges this idea, Kron threatens him. Aladar races back to the others. Although he'd like to stay with Neera and the Herd, he won't leave the misfits.

They are soon distanced from the Herd.

Beautiful Neera, who reveals her heart and kindness.

THIS PAGE:
Production stills.

"The broader acting of her body was a challenge too, because she's got to act feminine—and yet she's a dinosaur. I tried to move her in a nice, fluid, graceful way, but there's a fine line between getting that and making it look too computery, too smooth."

Julianna Margulies provides Neera's voice. "I had wanted to get Julianna for *The Hunchback of Notre Dame*," Lambert says. "*ER* had just started and she had won an Emmy Award and her then-agent said, 'Absolutely not.'

"Her name came up again for *Dinosaur*, and I found that she had switched agencies. I called the new agent, and she came in the next day!"

Margulies went to extremes to give an authentic performance as an iguanadon. "Well, she's the first character I've ever played where I had to gain two tons. I ate a lot of pizza. Did a lot of starches, that helped," the actress laughs.

Margulies was excited about providing Neera's voice, but wasn't expecting the challenges she faced in a new kind of acting. "The hard part comes when the director says, 'Remember, you're 25 feet long, and you weigh two tons, and you're in the middle of a herd, running.' All of a sudden, you're thinking, 'Well, how

do I do that?' You try as many times as you can, and whichever one works, they use. We're all in it together, and they say, 'Okay, just try to sound like a dinosaur.' I mean, what are you gonna do?" Margulies chuckles.

"When Julianna auditioned, we all fell in love with her, we hired her, and that was that. She's lovely, she's the most beautiful creature. I mean, she's so beautiful, I think Ralph Zondag fainted."

ABOVE: *Production stills.*

RIGHT: *Orthographic drawings of Neera by David Krentz.*

THE FASTEST DINOSAUR, THE OSTRICH-LIKE ORNITHOMIMINNEE ("BIRD MIMIC") IS ESTIMATED TO HAVE RUN AT SPEEDS UP TO 50 MILES PER HOUR.

DON'T-CONTRADICT-ME EEMA

Eema is an old, slow-moving styracosaur who has been with Kron's Herd for as long as she can remember. Although warm and good-natured, she also has a definite attitude when it comes to those who may challenge her experience.

Supervising animator Gregory Griffith says, "Eema is walking down the road toward its end. She can see it, and she's not particularly happy about it. But she's not a fearful character at all. I like that about her."

Griffith found the same challenge animating Eema that his colleagues did, with an additional detail. "She's the size of a minivan, but because of her age, her motion is quite limited even compared to the other dinosaur characters in the film."

In seeking ways to create Eema's character in motion, Griffith found a model in his own home. "Using my old dog, Eli, who had hip dysplasia, as a guide, I took a generic styracosaur model and created a stiff, arthritic walk motion for this generic model that worked quite well.

"Both as an element of her character and as the function of her design, Eema is not a creature that can do a whole lot more than shamble along, and not just only in her locomotion—it also affects her acting.

"She has this immense head. Not only does the size of her head place physical constraints on the believability of what she can do with it, but it doesn't fit into the frame very well. So I have deliberately constricted myself with Eema. I get as much as I can out of very small, simple gestures. One of the things that I introduced in Eema is a little defiant neck snap. It's a cocky head gesture that says, 'Don't contradict me.' That came from both the attitude of Eema's character, and from the voice performance of Della Reese."

"Tom Schumacher came up with Della," Lambert says. "He said, 'Try to get Della Reese. She's got a great voice and she'll give the character an instant and likeable read.'"

"Della brings a marvelous voice," Griffith simply states. "The quality of her voice is extraordinary. She is very aware of that and doesn't feel the need to layer a whole lotta stuff over the top. That voice, and a singular strong attitude, are

Fiesty Eema: a slow and stubborn styracosaur.

ABOVE: *Maquette of Eema by Michael Jones.*

OPPOSITE: *Production still.*

sufficient to carry the performance. She has a
marvelous instrument and it's a delight to
listen to and work with. Her performance is
constrained, yet very direct. It's not the least bit
withheld or searching."

"I never really saw her as a dinosaur," says Reese.
"I see her as an entity who has gone through some
of the things that I go through every day in this
process of living, and how she feels about it, and
her attitude toward it, that's what I was after."

Reese also saw the story of *Dinosaur* writ large.
"There's love and laughter, there's compassion and
tenderness, there's friendship and warmth, there's
mother-love and son-love, and the belligerence of
evil that is conquered. It's a very large palette."

BAYLENE—DIGNIFIED WALLS OF MEAT

Baylene is an elegant, elderly brachiosaur who is every inch a dignified lady. Like many a well-mannered matron, she is a displaced aristocrat in an unsympathetic world, an innocent forced into the brutal migration of a herd. She cares deeply for Eema, who has taken care of her ever since her arrival. Despite her large size, Baylene is timid and ill-prepared to survive the journey to the Nesting Grounds. But somewhere deep inside her burns a strong and courageous spirit that surfaces when Aladar loses hope on his quest.

Supervising animator Mike Belzer describes Baylene as "a sixty-five-year-old brachiosaur who has seen the world, been around—a matriarch who is the last of her kind. She feels out of place because she's being thrust into a herd, and can't quite keep up with the rest of them. She's one of the misfits in the back. She has a strength, but her reserve and dignity always come through."

Much of Baylene's dignity comes from a brilliant piece of voice casting—Joan Plowright. "I have to be honest with you, that's another one from the brain of Tom Schumacher," Lambert admits. "Tom came up with Joan Plowright and said, 'Make Baylene British and fussy.' Sure, Tom. Then, God bless her, she wanted to do it—how lucky did we get?"

"One of the most magical things about Baylene and Eema centers around the contrast of two voices, Joan Plowright and Della Reese," asserts Schumacher. "The way they care for each other in the film is one of my favorite things. They are clearly so different in every way, save for their present circumstances which bond them."

"When Joan Plowright was cast," Belzer says, "the floodgates opened. As is so often the case with animation, you have the idea of the character, but a good actor can give so much to that character. And with Joan, she's such a presence and her voice has such great qualities that it's a playground of ideas. When she talks, there's so much to grab hold of."

"Are pearls falling out of that character's mouth?" Lambert asks. "No. But it's Joan Plowright as a dinosaur, and that's funny. It's Joan Plowright, and how bitchin' is that?"

"How does one prepare to play a dinosaur?" Plowright muses. The actress first looked at drawings and models of Baylene and began to create the character in her mind based on a physicality. "I saw this huge dinosaur with a very, very long neck stretching up to the sky, and these gentle

eyes, and I began to think, 'Oh yes, she's a bit aloof, a bit shy, fundamentally gentle—though she looks as though she has enormous strength. That's how I began . . . looking at her from a picture and then letting her seep into my brain."

Animating Baylene was a departure for Belzer, whose background is primarily in stop-motion. "This whole process was different for me, because in stop-motion you supervise sequences, not characters. People ask, 'Who did you animate in *The Nightmare Before Christmas*?' Well, I animated all the characters in an individual scene, but here the idea is to supervise a single character's performance throughout the film.

"With Baylene, it was 'walls of meat' and 'head on a stick,'" Belzer laughs. "She's seventy feet long, and fifty feet tall. She's even been a background plate a couple of times—no sky, just Baylene. That's 'walls of meat'. There's a couple of scenes where we get some good body motion in her, but by and large, the camera angles just aren't wide enough to catch the whole thing. Because her neck is so long, in a lot of shots she cranes down into frame—this big head on a stick.

Belzer began Baylene by studying what he could. "There's no living beast on this planet near that size. I went to the zoo and these elephants would hardly move, even to eat, so I asked Pam

ABOVE: *Character development art of Baylene by David Krentz.*

BELOW: *Production stills.*

[Marsden] if we could rent an elephant for an afternoon. A group of us went, took notes, and videotaped it. I even got to ride the elephant at the end of the day. I also looked at building sites with these huge cranes, just to get a feeling of scale and weight. You have to dance that fine line between reality and a cartoon, and that's been the real challenge for a lot of us.

"We naturally relied on facial animation a great deal," Belzer continues. "I was told that the muscle structure I had in the brachiosaur was far more complex than what the real brachiosaur had. There was a very simple muscle structure under their faces. I'm sure a lot of paleontologists will question things that we've done. But more than scientific veracity, I'm interested in what looks right and what's believable, and what's fun for the character."

Url: the pet ankylosaur.

ABOVE: *Production still.*

BOTTOM LEFT: *Character development by David Krentz.*

URL—DINO'S BEST FRIEND

Url is a lovable ankylosaur who acts remarkably like a loyal family dog. He doesn't take a liking to just anyone, and astonishes both Eema and Baylene when he's instantly drawn to Aladar.

Belzer continues, "Url's the little wet-dog character who is always following Baylene. Brian Green did most of the animation with this character, but I was able to work with him, since Url is around Baylene a lot. The contrast between the sizes was a real treat. When it gets a little too heavy—no pun intended—to animate Baylene, there's Url to bounce back on and mess around with. Url hopping around like a little puppy dog is so much fun."

THE HERD CHARACTERS

On any film of the epic scale of *Dinosaur,* the sweeping visual nature of the film is supported by the legendary "cast of thousands." With the characters in the Herd, special attention was paid to supporting the realism of the rest of the film, and also to treating the group as an important character in and of itself. The supervision of the Herd characters was the responsibility of Atsushi Sato, who came from his native Japan to California in search of a "Hollywood Dream," that actually became a reality—and one of the many engaging success stories of *Dinosaur.*

"I wanted to work in film, that's why I moved to L.A. When I came to L.A., I had two companies in mind—one was Disney, the other was ILM. I was lucky to be hired by Disney. I was really excited to be hired by the Disney animation department. I was a part of Hollywood," Sato shyly states.

Sato was initially quite nervous about his assignment, since he had limited experience in CG animation—and even less experience in hand-drawn animation.

"I started as a trainee in 1996. I thought I'd have to study animation by myself. Then the company put me in a five-month training course called 'intensive training.' I got *paid* to study animation!"

Over the course of three years, Sato proved his mettle, being promoted at every review until he was finally made Supervising Animator of the Herd characters, carnotaurs, and raptors.

Sato is modest, but obviously proud of his experience on *Dinosaur*. "Since this is my first film project, I'm just excited to see the film in a theater with the audience. The look of the picture is so unique. It's not just a live-action. It's not just animation. I like that."

ABOVE AND RIGHT:
Production stills.

The End of the Story

Later that evening, carnotaurs arrive at the watering hole. After they drink, they continue to track the Herd. As Aladar, the lemurs, and the misfits try to keep up, Aladar rallies their spirits for the journey.

Aladar's group comes upon the wounded Bruton. He is seriously hurt, and can't keep up with the Herd. Eema recognizes the wounds. Carnotaur! The misfits are now afraid. Aladar tries to get Bruton to join them, but he refuses. As a storm approaches they seek shelter in a nearby cave.

Reluctantly, Bruton joins them. In the relative safety of the cave, everyone relaxes. Plio finds a plant to medicate Bruton's wounds. Bruton tries to understand the camaraderie and compassion that Aladar inspires in the misfits.

A short time later, Bruton wakes everyone up—carnotaurs lurk just outside the cave. As they try to escape, the noise alerts the predators, who smash into the cave after them. Bruton bravely rescues Aladar and fights the carnotaurs. One of the carnotaurs is killed but, unfortunately, so is Bruton.

As Kron's Herd continues its difficult trek toward the Nesting Grounds, the orphaned dinosaurs struggle to keep up. One collapses, exhausted. Inspired by Aladar, Neera tells the orphans that she won't let them get left behind.

Aladar, the lemurs, and the misfits march deeper into the cave until Zini finds a small way out. Too small. Aladar tries to push through the opening, but the wall collapses, closing them off completely. Aladar loses hope. Baylene chastises him for giving up—then she takes charge, pushing her way through a wall of rock. With renewed spirit, Aladar joins her. Together they push through the wall and find themselves, unexpectedly, at the Nesting Grounds.

Elated in their success, Aladar awaits the arrival of Kron's Herd, and especially Neera, but the Herd discovers their usual entrance to the Nesting Grounds is blocked by a massive rock slide. In spite of the danger, Kron decides that they will climb the rocks, and Aladar rushes from the safety of the valley to help the Herd.

Kron tries to drive the Herd up the rock slide. Some tumble down, injured. Aladar races to the Herd, shouting that he's found another way into the Nesting Grounds. The Herd starts to break rank, peeling away from Kron toward Aladar.

When Neera joins them, Kron viciously attacks Aladar, who is able to hold his own.

As the Herd begins to follow Aladar, a nearby roar distracts them, and they turn to see a carnotaur charging in their direction. Aladar tells the Herd to not run away but instead to join together against the carnotaur. Confused by their actions, the carnotaur turns its attention toward Kron, who is still trying to climb the rock slide. It attacks Kron, who is severely wounded. Aladar comes to his rescue and pushes the carnotaur to its death, but he is too late—Kron perishes. Joined by Neera, Aladar leads the Herd toward the valley.

"The art of progress is to preserve order amid change, and to preserve change amid order." —Alfred North Whitehead

A year later, the lemurs and misfits gather around a nest of unhatched eggs and eagerly wait with the proud parents, Aladar and Neera, the birth of the new generation. They bellow out in joy, joined by other Herd members throughout the valley.

OPPOSITE: *Aladar confronts the carnotaur. Production still.*

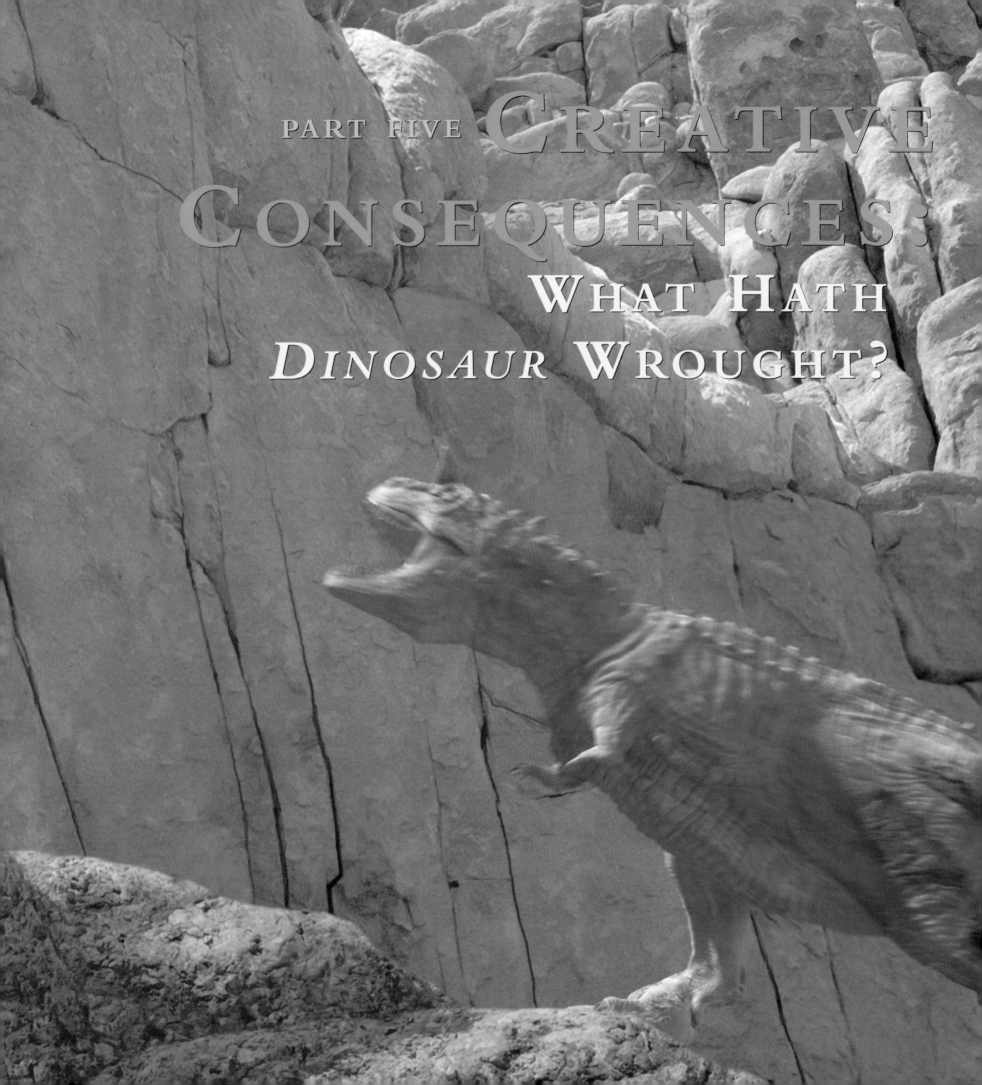

PART FIVE CREATIVE
CONSEQUENCES:
WHAT HATH
DINOSAUR WROUGHT?

STRUGGLING TOWARD THE HORIZON

After a staggering amount of time in development, with hundreds of production roles, dozens of artists, an ever evolving storyline and cast of characters, and

"Every day you may make progress. Every step may be fruitful. Yet there will stretch out before you an ever-lengthening, ever-ascending, ever-improving path. You know you will never get to the end of the journey. But this, so far from discouraging, only adds to the joy and glory of the climb." —Sir Winston Churchill

engineers and technicians who'd toiled without rest, they still weren't finished with *Dinosaur*.

"It's the classic thing of packing ten pounds of stuff into a five-pound bag," admits digital effects supervisor Neil Eskuri. "Such is the nature of innovation. One innovation inevitably leads to the need to alter or innovate at the next level."

"You can get real ticked off," Gavin says, "or you can be grateful to work here at Disney, where the commitment to the medium allows . . . well, demands, that we keep going."

PRECEDING PAGES: *The carnotaur chases Kron up the rock slide and to his death. Production still.*

RIGHT: *Production still.*

"Getting the animation performance nailed is a big step, a giant step," Marsden says. "But on this project, it's a lot like we're in the theater, we're on the stage, rehearsal is done, and now we move on to get ready for opening night. We have to add costuming, and wigs and makeup, and final lighting and set dressing, and a lot of the nuance that really pulls a show together for the audience."

AUTOMATIC MUSCULATURE

Once the animation process is complete, the physical attributes of a live animal are added in a groundbreaking system.

Director Leighton wanted a way to give the characters skin and muscles after the animation was done—he didn't want the animators to have to animate every muscle and fuss with every piece of skin that moved. The idea was to make the process as automatic as possible.

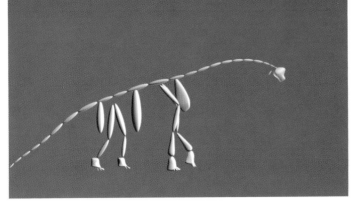

Other artists had attempted to build a similar system, but few had taken it as far as the creative team needed it to go. Most other productions had muscles built in as part of the skin.

"You could get musclelike looks to things," Sean Phillips says, "but it was difficult. If you were making a movie with fifty effects shots in it, you wouldn't have built our muscle and skin system. But we knew we had 2,500 shots coming at us, so it was worth spending some time up front to create a system that would be a little bit more automatic for getting muscle bulges and the like."

"We wanted musculature that moved independently of the skin, but where the skin acted like skin, elastic over the top," Jim Hillin says. "Making sure that you'd see muscles bulge underneath the skin independent of the skin movement. So, we came up with this huge software system that would put all the muscles underneath the skin and attach the skin to the bones, but not completely, so that it looked much more real."

SKIN POINTS, FIND YOUR BUDDIES!

"We got an idea that from the neutral position of the character in a 'stand at ease' pose," Phillips explains. "We would calibrate every point in the skin to the piece of the muscle that it was closest to. The muscle set, regardless of how it was made, would turn into little polygons, and every point in the skin found its little buddy polygon and said, 'Okay, I'm gonna stick to this.' Now the

THIS PAGE: *This series of images illustrates the "automatic" skin and muscle system developed by the* Dinosaur *team.*

BERNARD PALISSY WAS BURNED AT THE STAKE IN 1589 FOR HIS BELIEF THAT FOSSILS WERE ONCE LIVING CREATURES.

character could move off into a pose, and the skin would maintain that relationship with that underlying polygon—not with polygons off somewhere else—and follow it.

"In some areas it worked really well, but in stretchy areas like shoulders and thighs, it tore apart somewhat. We knew it would do that," Phillips admits, "but the real magic is that after that initial position, the skin turned into a spring-mesh system. It's the difference between having a cotton shirt and a Lycra shirt on. In the neutral pose, you get cotton shirt-looking skin, then we'd run this spring-mesh system on the skin and it would tighten everything up, and all the points would pull on each other and smooth out the kinks. The only major problem is that it had a tendency to smooth out the detail that the modelers painstakingly built in."

JIGGLY BITS AND RIPPLY BITS

"Now, looking at that motion in action," Phillips continues, "the other thing we realized we needed was the jiggling."

"If there was fatty tissue, like you see on an elephant," Hillin adds, "you would see that kind of motion in our final dinosaur model, too—and the bigger the animal is, the more of that there is."

"We knew that was something that we wouldn't have time to animate individually on each scene," Phillips says. "But we thought we could build it into the system to do it procedurally.

"It was amazing when we first got it working. The simplest motion—an arm bending up and down—suddenly became much more organic and real-looking when we got some of that jiggling happening in there. It happens on two levels: in the muscles and then on the skin. So we get a gross large movement in the muscle and then the subtle little ripply bits in the skin," Phillips says.

"In the end, when you're looking at the character, it's the jiggling in there that really sells it."

KICK OFF YOUR JIGGLE

Some of the animators learned what the skin and muscles could do, and adjusted their animation performance to take advantage of it. Phillips says, "One of the things we learned about is called rotational inertia. If you see an elephant take a step forward and put his leg down, the ripple doesn't just move up and down horizontally, it twists. On Baylene we added in controls for the animators to duplicate this rotational twist."

"We put some additional things on the characters as well, under the chin and stuff, so when the character inherently reacts to a sudden change in speed or direction, you had something to . . . kick off your jiggle."

AND THAT'S FINAL!

In addition to applying the "automatic" motion, there is a final refinement to the character performance known as character finaling. "All the skin and muscle subtleties were applied in the character finaling department," says Leighton. "Included in that department was a small army of asistant animators who were responsible for the vast amount of clean-up tasks needed—from animating secondary or "follow through" objects (like lemur tails), to making sure that all the characters were "married" to the backgrounds and each other—so that there was no visual relative slipping and sliding. Given the scale of this show, their efforts were nothing short of herculean."

ABOVE: *The arrows indicate the animation controls that were added to "roll" the bones and trigger rotational inertia.*

111

GRASS: THE GREATEST THING SINCE THE INVENTION OF ... FUR?

Necessity is the mother of invention, and many innovations on *Dinosaur* proved the adage true. Neil Eskuri recalls one example. "When we finally got to the valley, we were looking at the plates and trying to figure out a way to make the interaction of the characters work on the ground, because the grass in the live-action plate was about two or three feet tall. It was something we'd thought about a couple of years ago, but we were so focused on other things that it fell off to the side. Plus, we were in the desert all the time, so there wasn't even a need for grass until we got to the valley.

"Several of us sat around looking at it, figuring out ways to do it. Finally, we said, 'Well, let's use the fur tool we made for the lemurs and make green fur.' It worked. We had seven different strains of grass, and we did a test of Eema walking along a plane. We put her in a background from that sequence and laid the grass on top.

"It looked better than the real grass, because it moved, and we could make it move any way we liked. It self-shadows and self-mats; it buckles down, so as the characters are walking through it they mat it down, and it stays matted down. Then, gradually, it can start to come up. It does everything we want it to do.

"It looked so amazing," Eskuri beams, "that the directors decided in all of the plates where we were going to have the grass, we would take out all the real (live-action) grass and put in the CG grass!"

ABOVE AND LEFT:

The animators used the computer fur tool instead of live-action techniques to create grass. By doing so, they were able to control the delicate movements of the grass as the dinosaurs walked through it. Production stills.

113

THESE PAGES: *The different lighting requirements of various scenes in* Dinosaur—*from above or below water to inside a cave or under a tree—were created by a computer menu system. Production stills.*

YOU LIGHT UP MY LIFE

Like live-action films, each scene in *Dinosaur* had to be lighted. The process of lighting in computer animation occurs far earlier in the production schedule that it does on most live-action films, making lighting more a part of production design.

The lighting crew creates the mood and ambiance of a shot using every imaginable lighting source that a live-action filmmaking crew might use—and more. The *Dinosaur* lighting crew, however, did not have to contend with heavy equipment, power sources, or gels. Everything was controlled with a computer menu system.

Lighting lead Chris Peterson came to *Dinosaur* with a stop-motion cameraman's background on films like *James and the Giant Peach* and Tim Burton's *The Nightmare Before Christmas.* "The thing that really got me interested in this project was the idea that they were going to shoot miniatures for the backgrounds. Then, they decided to shoot the live-action background plates, so I was unsure if I was going to fit in. Carolyn Soper called and told me 'We would like to use your talents, and we'll train you with the tools.' So I tried to bring my expertise into a whole new medium.

"At first, I was trying to get a conception of what the images were about; how to light them to look realistic. I think that was the biggest challenge in the beginning. I'm used to being on a soundstage where you put up a bounce card and get this soft wash of light.

"I didn't know enough about all the technical details of what it takes to make a surface reflect light the way it should," Peterson explains. "With the software, there's a huge line of code that determines that. As I became more comfortable with the 'virtual stage,' I realized that CG is really a lot of mimics, or 'cheats,' of visual perception. A big part of learning the tools was learning to utilize these tools to get that cheat across.

"The medium offers an array of options: a key light, a fill value, and any kind of specialty lights we want to put in there as kickers, highlights, and special leafings to bring up eyes.

"It definitely evolved as we went along. We made design decisions based on the story. At times, you want to feel like *National Geographic*, other times you want to get a little more theatrical to get a moment. Just like you do with any other film, you light it to get what the scene requires, whether you're being theatrical or documentary."

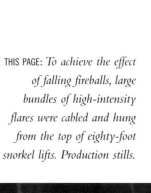

THIS PAGE: *To achieve the effect of falling fireballs, large bundles of high-intensity flares were cabled and hung from the top of eighty-foot snorkel lifts. Production stills.*

WELL, ISN'T THAT SPECIAL...EFFECTS

In addition to the characters and their environments, every atmospheric effect in *Dinosaur*—water, smoke, fire, and fog among them—had to be computer-enhanced or computer-generated. Meeting these challenges required a variety of special techniques.

COMPOSE YOURSELF

Compositing is the act of assembling the various levels of the computer-generated frame (background, foreground, character) into each single frame of film at high resolution, in preparation for printing the image onto motion picture film. "The big deal here was that the computer stuff can look infinitely more sharp than anything we ever shoot on camera, so how do you get the two to go together?" says Neil Eskuri. "It's not supposed to look like a computer here, a background in Hawaii there, a soundstage over in Burbank there. You're not supposed to see that stuff, or it falls apart right in front of the audience. So that's the challenge of compositing, to try to take those disparate elements and make them look like they were shot same day, same camera."

Eskuri elaborates, "In order to do that, we shot everything in the background plate as sharp as possible, so we could manipulate it later. Then we came up with techniques to give our rendered characters a sense of depth. We tried to look at the whole film from the viewpoint of a six-foot-tall human being. We had a lot of three-quarter upshots, where we were looking at the legs or feet of the characters. And we were shooting with the equivalent of a 50-millimeter lens—there's that sense of depth. We had an area of focus with everything else falling off into more of a blur. Those two tools alone gave the sense that the two worlds were in the same environment at the same time."

"Then, we added some 'cinematic vernaculars' into the mix," Marsden adds. "Some lens flares and motion blur for an additional layer of photorealism."

THIS PAGE: *Putting it all together: live-action backgrounds and foregrounds need to be composed with computer-generated characters. Production stills.*

Every scene in Dinosaur required many stages and the combination of many elements:
THIS PAGE AND BOTTOM RIGHT, COUNTERCLOCKWISE FROM LEFT: *A live-action background plate; color is added to background shot; rough animation of characters; character-finaling animation and live-action images are combined; computer-generated ripples are added to the water; the final result (above) contains real splashes and computer-generated ripples in the water.*

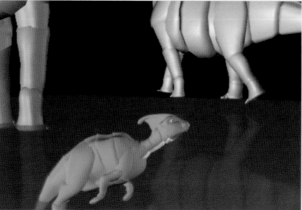

MMMMM ... DINOSAUR LAYER CAKE

Compositing usually involves the marriage of dozens of different elements.

Eskuri says, "Combining 70 elements is a good-size scene, but a big number of our scenes have many more: shadow layers, color correction layers, and of course, the character layers—then the tonal layers. And all of those add up. But I think that's required for the realism of this film."

Do audiences really notice all of this detail? Eskuri's answer is, surprisingly, "No, they don't. But if there wasn't a shadow there, you'd sense it. If it wasn't moving correctly, or if it was strobing, you'd sense it. Generally speaking, we take the time to make sure that it's right because first, no film has ever been made like this. Second, this is a Disney picture, and we have a level of quality that we have to achieve. If we don't hit it, we go back and do it again."

AWAY WE GO: OUTPUT TO FILM

The final phase of the assembly of the visual element of *Dinosaur* is when the digital image is transferred to motion picture film for release to theaters.

This step is profoundly intricate. Eskuri explains the complexities: "Sending it to the film recorder? Put out your film request, give your files, and away it goes. That's it, for the most part, pretty cut and dried. The camera department is extremely good at making sure that the color balances, the film stocks, and all of that are consistent. But putting all those elements together is very tedious. You have to look at every frame of every scene over and over again."

How many is "over and over"? Eskuri muses, "I wouldn't be surprised if we look at every scene, no matter how long or short—the longest

ABOVE: *A gliding lizard finds his lunch. Production still.*

119

is 834 frames, the shortest is twelve frames—a couple hundred times each to make sure that every little thing is just right. Granted, there are little pops that go through, or a shadow that's not quite the right density, or a map that is there—or isn't there—for one frame. Some of those things might get past you. But when you're watching it within the continuity of the film, you wouldn't even notice them.

"Putting all of those pieces together,—and we've got more than 1,300 of them—making sure that they all land in the right spot, is like a giant Rubik's Cube. That part I find fascinating, and the artists who do that are very good. Fortunately!"

HEY, *DINOSAUR* TEAM! YOU'VE JUST FINISHED ONE OF THE MOST COMPLICATED MOVIES IN HISTORY! WHAT ARE YOU GOING TO DO NOW?

Terry Moews, who'd had spent more than a year supervising the background plate shoots for the film, describes his favorite *Dinosaur* memory: "Sitting in the basket of a forty-five-foot crane arm at 4:30 A.M., with the temperature at forty-five degrees, under a rain system, in the middle of the desert, as I cut the camera on the last plate shot taken by the first unit after a nineteen-month schedule."

RIGHT: *The* Dinosaur *journey.*
Production still.

This project had gone on for a very long time, even for the usually generous schedule of an animated feature. Those with a background in CGI effects are used to short, shot-based schedules, where a "long" project is one that goes on for five months. *Dinosaur* was in active production for nearly five years.

Neil Eskuri admits that a positive outlook helps on a very long project like *Dinosaur*. "It's fun when it works. There have only been two places in my career where I come into work thinking, 'What am I going to see today?' and this is one of them. Sure, it's been tough, but it's also been a lot of, 'Wow! Look at this! Can you imagine? Have you ever seen anything like this before?'"

SMORGASBORD OF TALENT

"This film was a challenge," supervising animator Larry White admits. "I'm one of the few 'traditional animation' people from Disney that actually came over here, trained, and stayed with it. They were bringing in people from different disciplines—from stop-motion and from the computer world. It was exciting for me to work with all these people from various working environments. We all brought something else to the picture. We were always trying out new ways of working together, skills, bringing a grab bag of tastes and approaches to the project. That was exciting."

LEFT: *Carnotaurs track the Herd. Production still.*

Eskuri's role as digital effects supervisor was one of two hats he wore. "I'm also the artistic coordinator for the show. I'm looking at how to keep a rein on the film to keep it from getting out of hand. That's a big part of my job, just getting the pipeline in place with the help of all departments. We were lucky—everybody realized that we were in the same boat, and we all pitched in and said 'We have to work together in order to make this thing work, because nobody has ever done this before.' I was working with a tremendous number of incredibly talented people."

Eskuri modestly admits, "I had lunch with Carolyn Soper one time. She said she liked me being on the show, that I was able to bring a lot of disparate personalities together. I looked at her and said, 'Quite frankly, Carolyn, I don't know what I'm doing, and I don't know how I'm doing it . . . whatever it is.'"

NEVER AGAIN!

"You ask one person, and they say, 'Well, we're never doing that again,'" Jim Hillin admits. "You ask another person and they say, 'We should make use of the technology and move it forward.' I think what's being said is 'We'll never do *Dinosaur* the way we did *Dinosaur* again.'"

"A lot of analogies have been given to this show: building a house from the outside in, or sailing an ocean voyage while you're building the ship," Neil Eskuri agrees. "That's all true. We

ABOVE: *Aladar comforts Neera as she mourns the death of her brother, Kron. Production still.*

didn't have a finished story, we didn't have a finished design, we didn't have a finished pipeline, we were still hiring people, yet we were making a movie. And guess what? We were learning and knocking hurdles over on a daily basis. Given the alternatives—doing nothing, or following instead of leading—we made the right choice."

"The way we jumped into this project was probably naïve, and we should be more prepared next time," Gavin concedes. "On the other hand, innovation requires risk, and great innovations do come from jumping in headfirst."

"I'm often asked what makes our work so different, yet so successful," Schumacher adds. "Among a thousand other things, I believe it is a commitment to the medium of animation and an ongoing exploration and examination of what constitutes that medium. This isn't my bright idea, or some dictum from Michael Eisner or Peter Schneider. It's greater than that, and goes to the heart of who we are as a company. We're in it for the long haul, and that allows us to take risks, and to screw up. It also allows us to succeed gloriously."

A LEGACY OF TECHNICAL INNOVATION

"I think Disney always does the newest thing, the next thing. They don't establish something that works and then work it to death," Trey Thomas says. "I think they want to do it and then let everyone else copy it as Disney moves on to the next thing. It's just kind of the Disney style. I can see a lot of the technology and software that's been developed here being useful in effects-type situations."

Hillin concurs. "We anticipated buying all the hardware and software. We knew we'd influence future animation, and no one wanted to make these decisions haphazardly. We built a huge infrastructure to do this movie knowing the next movie probably will use it."

A PROGRESSION OF TECHNICAL INNOVATION

"Other shows already are using what we've got," Hillin says. "Other shows are seeing what we've done on our picture and saying, 'I've gotta have that for my movie.'

"Early on in CG here, we saw that each show would have its own individual needs, and once the show was over, we didn't want the tools to go away and be locked up in a vault," Hillin recalls. "On *The Rescuers Down Under*, Scott Johnson and Andrew Turner created a system for getting McLeach's truck to go over the terrain. That later became the basis of software for the wildebeest stampede in *The Lion King* to follow the terrain and go over the side. That same system was

124

ABOVE: *The Herd looks for hope and survival. Production still.*

further developed to become crowds of people in *The Hunchback of Notre Dame.*

"That system was then rewritten again to become the herds of dinosaurs, with all of their needs, specific to our movie. It's just progressing, progressing, progressing. So in ten years, what started as a simple piece of software has now become a much more complex system.

"I find it very rewarding. Disney isn't afraid of just taking a good idea, going off, and seeing what comes of it. We don't know if we're going to get any kind of return on it, but I think it gives artists some freedom of expression, which Disney allows absolutely. That in turn gives a sense of fearless innovation, 'let's try another style, let's try another way of animating or doing backgrounds'—or whatever it might be."

WORKING ON A MILESTONE

Trey Thomas looks at *Dinosaur* with sentimentality. "In my mind, I don't care about box office, it's what you think of the film twenty years later. It's nice to make money, but the fact is you're making something that you should be proud of for years to come."

"Disney has learned a tremendous amount on this," reflects Neil Eskuri. "They've built a phenomenal foundation, which I hope springboards into more projects. I feel very honored to be part of this show. Being part of a film that is this different, this realistic, may be the biggest reward. It is the highest point of my career. Two and one-half years ago, when Tom Schumacher saw our very first successful lip sync, he was stunned. He said, 'This is going to be one of those shows that will have been great to have worked on.' He's right. It was painful, but when it's done we can look at it and say, 'You know, I worked on that.'"

BELOW: *Happy endings at the Nesting Grounds: a new generation is born. Production still.*

EPILOGUE:
THE SECRET LAB

In November of 1999, The Walt Disney Company announced the merger of the Digital Studio that created *Dinosaur* with Dream Quest Images, a Simi Valley visual effects house that Disney had purchased in May of 1996. This new business will be known, or rather unknown, as The Secret Lab. Primarily located in the Northside Studio where *Dinosaur* was made, more than 400 digital artists of TSL will produce CGI character animation, visual effects for live-action projects, and computer animation features.

"It's an auspicious digital debut from the great gray granddaddy of animation," Paula Parisi exulted in the pages of *The Hollywood Reporter* on the unveiling of The Secret Lab. "Now, the firm adds another notch to Hollywood history, staking out its turf on the silicon frontier that is the future of the medium."

ABOVE: *Plio and Yar watch a dinosaur egg hatch for the second time. Production still.*

ACKNOWLEDGMENTS

Eternal thanks go to Peter Schneider, chairman of The Walt Disney Studios, and to Thomas Schumacher, president of Walt Disney Feature Animation, for their support and encouragement. Thanks in turn to Peter's assistant, Stacie Iverson, and to Tom's assistant, Pam Waterman; and to Royal Riedinger, for their help on this project.

I am also appreciative to Michael Eisner for the benefit of his time and insight, to John Dreyer for establishing that access, and to Jody Dreyer, just because.

Thanks to the Dinosaur production team—specifically to (in alphabetical order) Mike Belzer, Baker Bloodworth, Eamonn Butler, Thom Enriquez, Bill Fletcher, Gregory Griffith, Larry Heidel, Neil Krepela, Eric Leighton, Cristy Maltese, Pam Marsden, Terry Moews, Chris Peterson, Sean Phillips, Serge Riou, Atsushi Sato, Trey Thomas, Larry White, and Ralph Zondag. I am especially thankful for the extra effort and additional detail and insight provided by Mark Anthony Austin, Neil Eskuri, Joel Fletcher, and Jim Hillin.

Laura Gross kindly provided interview material for the voice cast and Peter Schneider, which proved vital.

Robert Tieman is, as usual, a terrific archivist and a terrific friend. To my other staunch supporters—Shawn Hayes, Dan Long, Armistead Maupin, Tim O'Day, Dave Walsh, Gilles C. Wheeler—I give my

"Change does not necessarily assure progress, but progress implacably requires change. Education is essential to change, for education creates both new wants and the ability to satisfy them." —Henry Steele Commager

There is only one Wendy Lefkon, and I am a lucky man to count her as a colleague and as a friend. I am grateful to associate editor, Rich Thomas, for his diligence and good humor. Sara Baysinger went beyond her editorial role and became my booster, cheerleader, and friend. And thanks to Monique Peterson for her keen editorial eye.

I am grateful to the talented people at Welcome Enterprises, especially Alice Wong; and designer Jon Glick, for both his art and his encouragement.

At Disney, Dhari Balvin, Jay Carducci, Andreas Deja, Kathleen Gavin, Ruth Lambert, Juliet Nees, and Todd Neilsen were helpful and important to this project, and I am always appreciative of the support and assistance of Howard Green in Walt Disney Pictures Publicity. Ed Squair in the Walt Disney Photo Archives performed his usual fine research, and is responsible for the archival illustrations in this book.

heartfelt appreciation. My family was there, as always: Evelyn Evich, Evelyn Kurtti; Ron, Joan, Jesse, and Darby Kurtti; Jerry Kurtti and Damien Conner; and Shawna Kurtti.

In my life apart from writing books, I work on an almost daily basis with a tight-knit team of true pros, and I treasure them and our work together. So to Susie Lee, Michael Pellerin, Eric Sanford, and Phil Savenick, my love and appreciation.

Finally, I owe the exciting, beautiful, and peaceful place in which I find myself in large part to the kindness, encouragement, and love of my very best friend, Kenneth Martinez.

—*Jeff Kurtti*

WALT DISNEY PICTURES
presents

DINOSAUR

Directed by   RALPH ZONDAG
   ERIC LEIGHTON

Producer   PAM MARSDEN

Co-Producer   BAKER BLOODWORTH

Screenplay by   JOHN HARRISON
   ROBERT NELSON JACOBS

Based on an Original
Screenplay by   WALON GREEN

Original Score
Composed by   JAMES NEWTON HOWARD

Editor   H. LEE PETERSON, A.C.E.

Production Designer   WALTER P. MARTISHIUS

Visual Effects
Supervisor   NEIL KREPELA, A.S.C.

Art Director   CRISTY MALTESE

Digital Effects
Supervisor   NEIL ESKURI

Story by   THOM ENRIQUEZ
   JOHN HARRISON
   ROBERT NELSON JACOBS
   RALPH ZONDAG

Production Managers   TAMARA BOUTCHER
   CAROLYN SOPER

Manager,
Digital Production   JINKO GOTOH

Associate Editor   MARK HESTER
Sound Designer &
Sound Supervisor   CHRISTOPHER BOYES

Executive Music Producer   CHRIS MONTAN

STORY

Director of Story   THOM ENRIQUEZ

Story Artists   DARRYL KIDDER
   ROY MEURIN
   FRANK NISSEN
   RAY SHENUSAY
   DICK ZONDAG

VISUAL DEVELOPMENT
& CHARACTER DESIGN

Artists   RICARDO DELGADO
   IAN S. GOODING
   MARK HALLETT
   DOUG HENDERSON
   DAVID KRENTZ

CHARACTER ANIMATION

ALADAR
Supervising Animator   MARK ANTHONY AUSTIN
Voice of Aladar   D.B. SWEENEY

Animators   JASON ANASTAS
   DARRIN BUTTERS
   JAY N. DAVIS
   CHADD FERRON
   AMY MCNAMARA
   ERIC STRAND

PLIO
Supervising Animator   TREY THOMAS
Voice of Plio   ALFRE WOODARD

Animators   GREG MAGUIRE
   SEAN MAHONEY
   LUCI NAPIER

YAR
Supervising Animator   TOM ROTH
Voice of Yar   OSSIE DAVIS

Animators   PETER LEPENIOTIS
   CHRISTOPHER OAKLEY

ZINI
Supervising Animator   BILL FLETCHER
Voice of Zini   MAX CASELLA

Animators   LES MAJOR
   YURIKO SENOO
   ALEX TYSOWSKY

SURI
Supervising Animator   LARRY WHITE
Voice of Suri   HAYDEN PANETTIERE

Animators   SHERYL SARDINA SACKETT
   HENRY SATO, JR.

KRON
Supervising Animator   EAMONN BUTLER
Voice of Kron   SAMUEL E. WRIGHT

Animators   DOUG BENNETT
   JASON RYAN

NEERA AND JUVENILE DINOSAURS
Supervising Animator   JOEL FLETCHER
Voice of Neera   JULIANNA MARGULIES

Animators   REBECCA WILSON BRESEE
   SANDRA MARIA GROENEVELD
   TONY SMEED

BRUTON
Supervising Animator   DICK ZONDAG
Voice of Bruton   PETER SIRAGUSA

Animator   OWEN KLATTE

BAYLENE & URL
Supervising Animator   MICHAEL BELZER
Voice of Baylene   JOAN PLOWRIGHT

Animator   BRIAN WESLEY GREEN

EEMA
Supervising Animator   GREGORY WILLIAM GRIFFITH
Voice of Eema   DELLA REESE

Animators   DARRIN BUTTS
   JAMES MICHAEL CROSSLEY
   ANGIE GLOCKA

CARNOTAURS & THE HERD
Supervising Animator   ATSUSHI SATO

Animators   BOBBY BECK
   STEPHEN A. BUCKLEY
   KENT BURTON
   CHRIS HURTT
   DON WALLER
   PAUL WOOD

ADDITIONAL ANIMATION

Animators   TOM GURNEY
   ETHAN MARAK
   NEIL RICHMOND

Lead Assistant Animator   THOMAS WEIGAND

Key Assistant Animators   LORI BENSON-NODA
   YANCY CALZADA
   MONIQUE DESCHAMPS
   LELAND J. HEPLER
   JASON WILLIAM WOLBERT
   GEORGE WONG

Assistant Animators   TIMOTHY ALBEE
   THERESA CLARK
   MARK DUVALL
   CHRIS EDWARDS
   DEREK FRIESENBORG
   JASON HERSCHAFT
   JON HOOPER
   LISA LIBUHA
   ALEXANDER MARK
   GAVIN MORAN
   RUDY RAIJMAKERS

   JOSH SCHERR
   MARK SCHREIBER
   THOMAS R. SMITH

SCENE FINALING

Effects Lighting
Supervisor   CHRIS PETERSON
Effects Compositing
Supervisor   JIM HILLIN

Supervising Effects
Animators   MICHAEL N. DAUGHERTY
   CURTIS A.J. EDWARDS
   SIMON O'CONNOR
   PATRICK ROBERTS

Lighting TDs/
Compositors/EFX Artists   CHARLES ANDERSON
   GRANT ANDERSON
   FLOYD CASEY
   D. WALLACE COLVARD
   ROBYN CRANE
   CHRISTIAN CUNNINGHAM
   EARL HUDDLESTON
   MICHAEL LEVINE
   JUNIKO MOODY
   WALLY SCHAAB
   LAURA SCHOLL
   KATHI SPENCER
   ADAM STARK
   KENJI SWEENEY
   ALESSANDRO TOMASSETTI
   WAYNE VINCENZI

Compositors/EFX Artists   ARTHUR ARGOTE
   YINA CHANG
   JIM H. GREEN
   JOAN KIM
   KEVIN KONEVAL
   IRINA MILOSLAVSKY
   ETHAN A. ORMSBY
   WINSTON QUITASOL
   ALIZA SOROTZKIN
   LISA M. TSE
   KATIE A. TUCKER

Lighting TDs/EFX Artists   TZYY WEI HUANG
   CHRIS HUMMEL
   ALESSANDRO JACOMINI
   SHANNA C. LIM
   ZSOLT KRAJCSIK
   BAUDOUIN STRUYE

Lighting TDs   JIM AUPPERLE
   RICHARD E. LEHMANN
   MATHIAS LORENZ
   STEVEN MCCURE
   TERRY MOEWS
   KYLE STRAWITZ

Compositors   JUDITH BELL
   BROOKS CAMPBELL
   FELICIANO DI GIORGIO
   LINDA HENRY
   ROBERT MROZOWSKI
   JANUARY NORDMAN

Assistant Lighting TD   ALFRED URRUTIA

Visual Design & Digital
Background Painting   KAREN DEJONG
   ALLEN GONZALES, S.O.C.
   ERIC S. MCLEAN

Additional Supervision   DENNIS BLAKEY
   KEN BRAIN
   MARK LASOFF
   MARY JANE TURNER

DIGITAL 2D PAINT & ROTO
Supervisor   SANDY HOUSTON

Artists   JACQUELINE ALLARD
   ELISSA BELLO
   MARCUS Y. CARTER
   CHRISTINE W. CRAM
   DOUG CRAM
   LISA A. FISHER
   KENT GORDON
   ALEXANDER LINGER
   STACIE MATHIESEN
   JENNIFER E. MURRAY
   DOLORES POPE
   BARBARA C. REED
   LUCY GREEN TAYLOR

MODEL DEVELOPMENT

Supervisor   SEAN PHILLIPS
Muscle & Skin TD Lead   DAVID OLIVER
Muscle & Skin TDs   JESUS CANAL TERES
   MARK EMPEY
   STEPHEN V. HWAN
   KAVITA KHOSLA
   MICHAEL KUEHN
   RAJ S. NAIKSATAM
   EDWIN NG
   RUSSELL L. SMITH

Character Motion
TD Lead   CANDICE CHINN
Character Motion TDs   HAGGAI GOLDFARB
   JACQUELINE GORDON
   SEAN LOCKE
   JAMES DALE POLK
Herd TDs   CRAIG CATON-LARGENT
   GLEN CLAYBROOK
   PETER MEGOW
Character Model Lead   BRUCE D. BUCKLEY
Associate Character
Model Lead   JAMES E. STAPP

Character Modelers   BRIAN JEFCOAT
   COREY SMITH
   DANIEL SZECKET
   JOE HING SHAN KWONG
Assistant Modelers   LYNN BASAS
   CHRISTOPHER COWAN
   GREG MARTIN
   DANIEL E. WANKET

Set & Prop Assistant
Modeler   MARK CHENG

SOFTWARE

Supervisor   JAY SLOAT

Dinosaur Muscle & Skin   DR. DONALD L. ALVAREZ
   ROSS KAMENY
   KEVIN RODGERS

Lemur Fur & Enveloping   MARK A. MCLAUGHLIN
   ERIC V. POWERS
   SERGI SAGAS-RICA

Modeling and Facial Tools   STEWART DICKSON
   DAVID REMBA
   MARK SWAIN
   DAVID TESCH
   XINMIN ZHAO

Animation and
Herding Tools   JEFFREY EDWARDS
   ÉRIC GERVAIS-DESPRÉS
   MOHIT KALLIANPUR
   HANNS-OSKAR PORR

LOOK DEVELOPMENT

Supervisor   L. CLIFF BRETT

Look Development TDs   ROBERT BEECH
   LAURENT CHARBONNEL
   MARK HAMMEL
   TAL LANCASTER
   RAMPRASAD SAMPATH
Character Painters   DARREN BEDWELL
   ESTHER FERRER-CARDONA
   CAROL HAYDEN
   MICHELLE LEE ROBINSON
   PAMELA SPERTUS
   CHARLES TAPPAN
Fur Stylist   CHARLES COLLADAY
Set & Prop Painter   HAMID RAHMANIAN

WORKBOOK

Supervisor   DAVID WOMERSLEY

Journeymen   DAVID KRENTZ
   RICK MOORE
   JIM SCHLENKER

3D Workbook Artists   CORY ROCCO FLORIMONTE
   TODD JAHNKE
   SEAN MATHIESEN
   ROBERT NEUMAN
   MICHAEL ORLANDO
   FAYE YEE

DIGITAL IMAGE PLANNING

Supervisor — KEVIN WILLMERING

Digital Image Planners — JEFFREY BAKSINSKI
JONATHAN GERBER
GREGG LUKOMSKI
JUSTIN KAMA MOIHA
MICHAEL A. RAMIREZ
JERRY SELLS
LAURIE TRACY
MICHELLE URBANO-JOHNSON
ERIC VIGNOLA

ASSISTANT PRODUCTION MANAGERS

Scene Finaling
Production Supervisor — NANCY SAMPSON

Story — JEFF DECKMAN
Editorial — TIMOTHY JASON SMITH
Production Design — LARRY HEIDEL
KRISTINA LONG
3D Workbook — JASON I. STRAHS
Software, Modeling &
Look Dev — KIM BOYLE
Visual EFX Editorial — TONY MATTHEWS
Digital Image Planning — SETH C. WALSH
BRIAN BEHLING
Animation — BARBARA T. LA BOUNTA
Sweatbox — LIANE ABEL DIETZ
Character Finaling — HEATHER MORIARTY HOBBS
Lighting & Compositing — FRED WEINBERG
Digital EFX — SUZI WATSON-JAEGER
Artics & Paint/
Digital Backgrounds — STEPHEN J. SHEA
Production — STACEY ERNST-CAMPBELL
PATRICK GOLIER
FRED HERRMAN
Florida — STEPHEN R. CRAIG

COORDINATORS
Communications — SERGE RIOU
Rendering — CHARLIE PUZZO
Scene Set Up — JOEY HUYNH

Administrative Managers — MARY WALSH
TANJA KNOBLICH

Manager, Disk Space
and Retakes — SHAWNE ZARUBICA
Assistant Manager,
Disk Space — LYNN MARIE GEPHART

EDITORIAL

1st Assistant Editor — CRAIG PAULSEN
Assistant Editors — KARL ARMSTRONG
ANNA M. SOLORIO-CATALANO
LISA DAVIS
Dialogue Readers — JAMES MELTON
HERMANN H. SCHMIDT

VISUAL FX EDITORIAL

Visual EFX Editor — THOMAS R. BRYANT

Visual EFX
Assistant Editors — ERIC WHITFIELD
JOYCE ARRASTIA
CRAIG CONWELL
ROBERT J. LEMOS
JULIE DOLE

Casting by — RUTH LAMBERT, C.S.A.
MARY HIDALGO

CAST
(in order of appearance)

Plio — ALFRE WOODARD
Yar — OSSIE DAVIS
Zini — MAX CASELLA
Suri — HAYDEN PANETTIERE
Aladar — D.B. SWEENEY
Kron — SAMUEL E. WRIGHT
Bruton — PETER SIRAGUSA
Neera — JULIANNA MARGULIES
Baylene — JOAN PLOWRIGHT
Eema — DELLA REESE

Additional Voices — MATT ADLER
SANDINA BAILOLAPE
EDIE LEHMANN BODDICKER
ZACHARY BOSTROM
CATHERINE CAVADINI
HOLLY DORFF
GREG FINLEY
JEFF FISCHER
BARBARA ILEY
DAVID ALLEN KRAMER
SUSAN STEVENS LOGAN
DAVID MCCHAREN
TRACY METRO
DARAN NORRIS
BOBBI PAGE
NOREEN REARDON
CHELSEA RUSSO
EVAN SABARA
AARON SPANN
MELANIE SPORE
ANDREA TAYLOR
JOHN WALCUTT
CAMILLE WINBUSH
BILLY WEST

A.D.R. Voice Casting by — BARBARA HARRIS

MUSIC

Orchestrations by — BRAD DECHTER
JEFF ATMAJIAN
JAMES NEWTON HOWARD

Electronic Score
Produced by — J.T. HILL
Score Conducted by — PETE ANTHONY

Choir Conducted by — PAUL SALAMUNOVICH
LEBO M
Vocals Arranged by — LEBO M
Score Recorded
and Mixed by — SHAWN MURPHY
Additional Engineering by — BILL SCHNEE

Supervising Music Editor — JIM WEIDMAN
Music Editor — DAVID OLSON
Director, Music
Production — ANDREW PAGE
Music Production
Manager — TOM MACDOUGALL
Music Production
Coordinator — DENIECE LAROCCA
Music Contractor — SANDY DE CRESCENT
Vocal Contractors — PHILLIP INGRAM
SALLY STEVENS
Music Preparation by — JO ANN KANE MUSIC SERVICE
Vocalists — JOSIE AIELLO
ALEXANDRA BROWN
LYNN DAVIS
JIM GILSTRAP
DORIAN HOLLEY
PHILLIP INGRAM
KUDISAN KAI
CHRISTINE LAFOND
DARRYL PHINNESSEE
LOUIS PRICE
LISBETH SCOTT
OREN WATERS
YVONNE WILLIAMS

PRODUCTION

Director of Production — DANA AXELROD
Director of Accounting — DENNIS PARK
Senior Manager of Camera — JOE JIULIANO

Production Controller — JAMES BURTON
Production Accountants — SUSAN ROYAL MCDONALD
ANTHONY R. REYES

Assistant Accountant — LORRIE CROSS-HOLGUIN
Accounting Assistant — JAMES OLIVIA

Assistant to Producer — SAJA KRISTINE SOKOL
Assistant to Co-Producer — DINA HARDY
Administrative Assistants — KAREN FAUST
MELISSA MCVICKER FREEMAN
PAULI MOSS
ROBERT JAMES MOSTACCI
DANA L. SOUTHERLAND

Production Assistants — ERIC ALVAREZ
JENNIFER BLECHSCHMID
IYAN MICHAEL BRUCE
JENNIFER CHO
AUDREY ELLEN CLARK
DWAYNE COLBERT
JASON COSLER
DAWNIE DESANTIS
KIMBERLY GORDON
BRYCE HALL
NICOLE P. HEARON
HEATHER ELISA HILL
JOHN R. HUGHES
JEANNINE JONES
KEVIN KENNARD
L. RHIANNON LEFFANTA
CINDY LEGGETT-FORD
DARA MCGARRY
MARY JO MILLER
PATRICK G. RAMOS
MARION KAY SHOAFF
TODD STRINGFIELD
JOHN TROSKO
TRACY WATADA
LISA MARIE WEBSTER
HEATHER WOLFE

Digital File Services — JOE PFENING

SCENE SET UP

Supervisor — GARY ALLAN PARKS

Administrators — ROBERT EDWARD BOAS
JASON CAMPBELL
STANLEY KWONG
SCOTT MANKEY
MICHAEL WILHELMI
MARK A. WILSON

Assistant Administrators — MARY THERESE CORGAN
ANDREW FULLER
KENNETH GIMPELSON
DERRICK HUCKVALE
AMY LAWSON
BRIAN SMITH
HEATHER D. WANG
JESSICA DARA WESTBROOK
RON WILLIAMS

RENDER I/O

Technical Lead — MARK M. TOKUNAGA

Administrators — JAMES COLBY BETTE
TOBY GALLO
CHRISTOPHER JAMES MILLER
ALAN A. PATEL
ANDREW R. RAMOS

Assistant Administrators — LORENZO RUSSEL BAMBINO
BRADLEY L. SMITH
DELLEON WEINS

DIGITAL FILM PRINTING AND SCANNING

Supervisor — CHRISTOPHER W. GEE

Camera Coordinator — STEPHANIE CLIFFORD
Color Timer — BRUCE TAUSCHER
Camera Operators — JOHN AARDAL
BILL AYLSWORTH
JOHN DERDERIAN
BILL FADNESS
MIKE LEHMAN
STAN MILLER
JENNIE KEPENEK MOUZIS
Quality Control — CHUCK WARREN
Additional Supervision — BRANDY HILL

POST PRODUCTION

Post Production
Supervisor — BÉRÉNICE LE MAITRE

Manager of
Post Production — SUE BEA MONTGOMERY
Post Production
Coordinator — MARISA JOHNSTON
Post Production
Administrator — HEATHERJANE SMITH
Video Coordinator — ROBERT H. BAGLEY
Post Production
Engineer — MICHAEL KENJI TOMIZAWA
Post Production Assistant — CORY HANSEN

Post Production Sound Services provided by
SKYWALKER SOUND, as a division of
Lucas Digital, Ltd.
Marin County, California

Supervising Sound
Editor — FRANK EULNER

ADR Supervisor — MICHELE PERRONE
Sound Effects Editors — ETHAN VAN DER RYN
SCOTT GUITTEAU
ANDREA GARD
Foley Editors — JIM LIKOWSKI
JOANNA LAURENT
JOHN VERBECK

Supervising Assistant
Sound Editor — ANDRÉ FENLEY
Assistant Sound Designer — BEAU BORDERS
Assistant Sound
Effects Editor — LISA CHINO

Foley Artists — DENNIE THORPE
JANA VANCE
Foley Mixer — TONY ECKERT
Foley Recordist — FRANK MEREL
Additional Field
Recordings — KATHY TURKO

Re-Recorded at — BUENA VISTA SOUND STUDIOS
Re-Recording Mixers — TERRY PORTER
MEL METCALFE
DEAN A. ZUPANCIC
CHRISTOPHER BOYES
Original Dialogue Mixer — DOC KANE
Additional Re-recording at — SKYWALKER SOUND

Dubbing Recordist — JUDY NORD
PDL — JEANNETTE CREMAROSA
Additional Dialogue
Recorded by — VINCE CARO
BRIAN REARDON
BRUCE BELL
Color Timer — TERRY CLABORN
Negative Cutters — BUENA VISTA NEGATIVE CUTTING
Main Title by — THE PICTURE MILL

Projection — BRIAN HENRY
KEN MOORE
Telecine — ROBERT J. HANSEN
Processing by — HOLLYWOOD FILM AND VIDEO
Prints by — TECHNICOLOR
Produced and
Distributed by — EASTMAN FILM

TECHNOLOGY

Manager, Software
Development — JOHN HENRY BROOKS
EDWIN R. LEONARD

Manager, Systems
Development — BEN CROY
Sr. Manager,
Technical Support — MICHAEL JEDLICKA

Manager, Media Group — THOMAS MOORE, JR.

Digital Systems
Design Team — STEVEN L. GROOM
MARK JANKINS
MARK KIMBALL
BRAD LOWMAN
SKOTTIE MILLER
NEIL OKAMOTO
SANDY SUNSERI
DOUG WHITE

Applications Software
Development & Support — ROGER BALART
JANET E. BERLIN
MICHAEL S. BLUM
BRENT BURLEY
MARK R. CARLSON
WILLIAM T. CARPENTER
NHI CASEY
BERNARD O. CEGUERRA
LAWRENCE CHAI
ELENA DRISKILL
HANK DRISKILL
ROBERT FALCO
STEVE HALL
JEFF HAMELUCK
GREGORY S. HEFLIN
JAMES P. HURRELL
KEVIN E. KEECH
MICHAEL R. KING
ERIC LARSEN
LAWRENCE LEE
CHRISTOPHER D. MIHALY
G. KEVIN MORGAN
MICHAEL NEVILLE
KYLE ODERMATT
MABEL LIM OKAMURA
FE ALCOMENDAS SAMALA
RAJESH K. SHARMA
MICHAEL TAKEYAMA
RASMUS TAMSTORF

ROY TURNER
JON Y. WADA
MARK WILKINS

Audio/Video and
Editorial Support
RICHARD M. BARNES
JOHN CEJKA
LOREN CHUN
JERRY A. EISENBERG
MASSIMILIANO GASPARRI
MARIA GOMEZ DE LIZARDO
ALEX HANSEN
MARY BETH KOCHIS
JOHN EDWARD LOPEZ
RON L. PURDY
SHELDON RIDDLES
JAMES A. SANDWEISS
JEFFERY L. SICKLER
BYRON STULTZ
MICHAEL ZAREMBSKI

Management Applications
Development
GLENN BELL
NORBERT FAERSTAIN
SEAN GOLDMAN
PAUL HILDEBRANDT
SHANNON HOWARD
DANNY JEWELL
DANIEL C. KIM
HANS KU
JOEL KURTZ
MICHAEL LARKIN
KEVIN A. MCGUIRE

Systems Development
GINA Y. CHEN
YAN CHEN
MICHAEL DEERKOSKI
SCOTT DOLIM
DALE DRUMMOND
DAVID PATRICK FLYNN
THOMAS GREER
MARC JORDAN
DAVID A. KARL
SUSANNA LENG
JAMES MACBURNEY
KEVIN P. NOLTE
ALLAN G. REMPEL
JOHN STIMSON
SCOTT S. TEREK
GEOFF W. THOMAS

Technical Support
MICHELLE BECK
MICHAEL C. BOLDS
ROBERTO A. CALVO
STEVE CARPENTER
MARGARET A. DECKER
ROSS DICKINSON
LYLY DO
DAVE M. DRULIAS
MARC FLEURY
BOBBY L. FOWLER, JR.
MARC FRANCOUER
SCOTT GARRETT
JASON HILKEY
BILL JAMES
AMINDRA JAYASINGHE
ROBERT JIMENEZ
CHRIS JOHNSON
MARYANN MCLEOD
ELIZABETH MEYER
JIM MEYER
KEN SANDBERG
MATTHEW F. SCHNITTKER
CARL VILLARETE
DEREK ELLIOTT WILSON

Additional Story
Material by
SHIRLEY PIERCE
RHETT REESE

ADDITIONAL STORY

Story Artists
JULIUS L. AGUIMATANG
KURT ANDERSON
JIM CAPOBIANCO
RICARDO DELGADO
ROBERT GIBBS
FRANCIS GLEBAS
BEN GLUCK
KIRK HANSON
DOUG HENDERSON
FRED LUCKY
FLOYD NORMAN
TOM SITO
MICHAEL SPOONER
TAMARA LUSHER STOCKER
OLIVER THOMAS
PETE VON SHOLLY

ADDITIONAL VISUAL DEVELOPMENT

Artists
BARRY ATKINSON
JIM AUPPERLE
HANS BACHER
JOHN BINDON
JUSTIN BRANDSTATER
MAREK BUCHWALD
BROOKS CAMPBELL
PETER CLARKE
GUY DEEL
PAUL FELIX
BRIAN FRANCZAK
MIKE GABRIEL
JEAN GILLMORE
DEREK GOGOL
ERIC GOLDBERG
VALERIE GRINEAU
CARLOS HUERTE
CAROLINE HU
TERRY ISAAC
BUCK LEWIS
RICK MAKI
SERGE MICHAELS
CRAIG MULLINS
PETER OEDEKOVEN
TINA PRICE
CRAIG PAUL
WILLIAM STOUT
CHRISTOPHE VACHER
MARCELO VIGNALI

Sculptors
MICHAEL FLOYD JONES
GARY STAAB

ADDITIONAL DIGITAL BACKGROUNDS

Digital Background
Painters
JUDITH BELL
ROBERT MROZOWSKI

SPIKES UP PLATE UNITS

Line Producer JAMES BURTON
Production Manager GERARD DINARDI

1ST UNIT

Visual FX Supervisor TERRY MOEWS
Directors of Photography STEVEN DOUGLAS SMITH
DAVE HARDBERGER
Additional VFX Supervisor RICHARD E. LEHMANN
Production Supervisors ANDREW FENADY
ELLEN RAPHAEL
ROBERT O'HAVER

CAMERA

1st Assistant Camera ERIC PETERSON
2nd Assistant Camera HEATHER RAE ROBERTS
JAMES PETE VANDER PLUM
Film Loader MICHELLE ZAJIC

GRIPS

Key Grip KIRT LEROUX HARDING
Best Boy Grip OTTO EMILIO BETANCOURT
Grips MARTIN "H" BAUKIND
MICHAEL BOGGS
DAVID J. DUMAS
JOHN DUMAS
MARIO ALBERTO SOTE VELOSO
RODNEY VETO
KEITH WHITEAKER
Safety Rigging DOUGLAS EDWARD MCDONALD
Safety Rigging &
Climbing Consultant MARK CHAPMAN

DINO CAM

Engineer & Operator DWAYNE MCCLINTOCK
Engineer STEVE T. KOSAKURA
Consultant EARL WIGGINS
Key Rigger CHRISTOPHER H. GILL
Best Boy Rigger CRAIG AINES
Rigger NEAL S. SHERIDAN
Machinists CHRISTOPHER SVANBERG
TOM TATE

ART DEPARTMENT

Set Decorator JEFFERY GANN MCMANUS
Art Department
Coordinator LAURA O'BRIAN
Greensmen BENNETT STEPHEN ANDREWS
STEPHEN FOLEY
MICHAEL GREGG
COREY MCNABB
FRANK MOREHEAD

SPECIAL EFX

Special Effects Supervisors ROBERT H. SPURLOCK
ROY L. GOODE
AL BROUSSARD
FX Crew ARCHIE K. AHUNA
STEPHEN L. HUMPHREY

SURVEY

Surveyor KIRK D. SCOTT
Survey Associate GARY BALIKIAN

ANIMATION

Animation Associates ERIC M. ALGREN
JACQUELINE I. TAYLOR
DONIQUE GRACE PATTON
Assistant Animation
Associate TERRANCE D. SHEARD
Animation Grip DAVID T. LARA

PRODUCTION

1st Assistant Directors TOM E. MILO
DONALD W. POQUETTE
2nd Assistant Directors CARA LEE MCCASTLAIN
KAYLEE MICHELLE BROWN
JENNIFER BOOTH

Supervising
Location Manager DOW GRIFFITH
Assistant
Location Manager RAINE MARIE HALL
Additional
Location Manager ROBERT M. BERKUS

Production Accountant JANE HARRISON
1st Assistant Accountants JULIE LAPRATH
CINDY ARNOLD
2nd Assistant Accountants KEVIN BOWE
TENA COTTON
DANITA COLE

Senior Production
Office Coordinator CHRISTOPHER A. DEBIEC
Production Office
Coordinators BONNIE JEAN FOLEY
LISA BETH GREENSPAN
Assistant Production
Coordinators JENNIFER JOY BLAIR
BRETT BOYDSTUN
LORI KORNGIEBEL
PETER LAWRENCE DRESS
Key Set
Production Assistant NATHANIEL W. CUSHMAN
Key Office
Production Assistant TROY DOUGLAS NIMMER
Production Assistants HILA AMIR
JASON BACHINSKI
MATTHEW M. COLLINS
JEREMY HOWARD KENDALL
FRANCIS GARY POWELL
BRIAN THOMAS READ
JEROME ROARK
WHITNEY STONE
CHRIS SULLIVAN

Nurse DEBORAH ANN SULLIVAN
Craft Service EVAN A. MCCALMON
MICHAEL G. RANDOLPH

Transportation Captains BRUCE LEONE
RICHARD D. JOHNSON
MYLES KAWAKAMI
JOHN PIERCE
FRED ROB ROBBINS

EXOTIC UNIT

Visual EFX Supervisor WALLACE SCHAAB
Director of Photography TIMOTHY HOUSEL

Production Supervisor NANCY MCCARTY
Key Grip GREG ROMERO
Production Coordinator MARK G. SOPER
Production Assistant JENNIFER JOHNSON

STAGE UNIT

Director of Photography KENNETH H. WIATRAK

1st Assistant Camera JOHN PASZKIEWICS
2nd Assistant Camera ARTHUR A.J. RAITANO
Special Effects Crew JOHN HARTIGAN
MIKE JOYCE
Gaffer JAMES J. TORGESON
Best Boy Lighting VINCENT G. EVERLY
Key Grip RANDY BERRETT
Grip MICHAEL SNYDER

Greensman RICHARD HENCH

Production Supervisor DIANA DE VRIES
1st Assistant Director SAMUEL J. HILL
Production Office
Coordinators RUTH IRVIN-HAUER
REGINA THOMPSON-WILLIAMSON
Nurse MARY LAHMAR MAHLER
Production Assistants RUSSELL BOLES
ANTHONY HARTMAN
EMMANUELLE-CLAUDE HEROX
JANET L. PRICE
MAURICE WILLIAMS

THE PRODUCERS WISH TO THANK:

MARK BLACKHAM
PAMELA SCHELL FOCHT
LESLIE WHITE
CAROLYN WILSON

ALTER PRODUCCIONES CINEMATOGRAFICAS, C.A.
THE CALIFORNIA FILM COMMISSION
THE AUSTRALIAN FILM COMISSION
THE LOS ANGELES COUNTY DEPARTMENT OF
PARKS AND RECREATION
UNITED STATES DEPARTMENT OF INTERIOR
BUREAU OF LAND MANAGEMENT
BO AND BEVERLY YARBOROUGH

A SPECIAL THANK YOU TO THE ENTIRE FEATURE
ANIMATION FAMILY FOR THEIR DEDICATION,
SUPPORT AND ENCOURAGEMENT IN THE
MAKING OF THIS FILM.

FILMED ON LOCATION IN:

AUSTRALIA
PORT CAMPBELL NATIONAL PARK

CALIFORNIA
DEATH VALLEY
DUMONT DUNES
LONE PINE
LOS ANGELES COUNTY ARBORETUM
RIDGECREST
SAN LUIS OBISPO
SAN SIMEON
TRONA PINNACLES

FLORIDA
SEMINOLE COUNTY

HAWAII
ISLANDS OF HAWAII AND KAUAI

VENEZUELA
EL PARQUE NACIONAL CANAIMA

WESTERN SAMOA
MATAUTU